MISSION: *impossible to* DENY

THE IMPOSSIBLE MISSION SERIES · Book Seven

JACKI DELECKI

MORE BOOKS BY JACKI DELECKI

CHAPTER ONE

Reeves Hewitt raced toward the light shining through the thick overhang. Butterfly blade in hand, he thrashed a path, desperate to escape the Colombian jungle.

He halted as the gorge suddenly materialized before him. His teammate, XChoco, barreled into him, throwing him forward. His heart thumped against his chest as he calculated the odds of crossing the wooden bridge swinging in the downdraft over a rushing tributary of the Amazon. Nature had carved an eight-hundred-foot cavern, creating a wind tunnel in the dense jungle. The bridge was held together with planks and rope and looked as if it hadn't been crossed since the Conquistadors plundered Colombia five centuries before.

Die by an eight-hundred-foot fall or be captured, tortured, and then killed by their pursuers? XChoco shoved him to get going. She wanted to make tracks from the bad guys as much as he did.

Muffled shouts in Spanish moved closer. He and XChoco had started on a mission to find a hidden *quipu* treasure the Inca's system of knots and strings used to record detailed data, information, and history.

They had been chased off their path by a pissed off mama jaguar, only to race smack into the middle of a drug runners camp. While being hounded by gun-toting druggers, he had made a wrong turn, taking them farther into the jungle and away from Leticia, the closest town in this part of the Colombian Rainforest.

He had to get XChoco across the bridge before the baddies caught up. His hands shook with the rush of adrenaline. The ropes might not tear, or the rotten wood might hold her weight if she could make it across in a hail of fire.

He signaled with his butterfly to cross quickly before the drug smugglers appeared. She would be an easy mark, swinging in the middle of the bridge. The sharp blade gleaming in the sunlight was his only protection against an enemy armed with AK-47s. How fair were those odds? He could stop a few to give her time to cross the hundred-foot span.

Midway across the bridge, XChoco twisted and signaled him to join her. She stopped and pulled out an M-4 from her backpack, then dropped to one knee on a skinny piece of wood and set up to give him a chance of surviving. How had he gotten lucky enough to have a smart-thinking and armed partner? He had chosen a knife in preparation, and she had chosen the Marine Corp's newest assault rifle. You had to love a partner who knew her guns.

He ran. His foot missed a plank, and he tripped. His heart and stomach plummeted as he swayed in the wind. The rat-tat of the AK-47 concussion reverberated over his head and against the canyon walls.

He was halfway when XChoco left her position to climb the cliff's steep incline. She fell to her stomach and positioned herself above the bridge to take the vantage point to cover him.

He sprinted to the end. One rifle against ten didn't add up to a happy outcome for either of them. With his blade, he worked frantically to saw through the rope. His chances of not being picked off—improbable. He was a sitting target, but XChoco wasn't. He had to sacrifice himself if one of them could make it out alive—no choice, really.

How humiliating it would be to have lost both his and XChoco's lives.

His ear drums were about to burst from XChoco's blast above him. She was ripping through the magazine as if there were no tomorrow.

A bastard aiming for XChoco hit the rock behind Reeves,

sending dust down on his head and briefly blinding him. Reeves didn't stop. With one last thwack, the rope tore apart, and the bridge swung wide before dropping with the weight of their pursuers. Now that they were halfway across, they teetered in a slow dance before falling into the long abyss. Their high-pitched screams as they hit the water resounded throughout the canyon.

He and XChoco had prevailed. Fueled with the rush of adrenaline coursing through him, he wanted to at least high-five his partner.

The lights flashed, and a "#1" zoomed across the video screen. He and XChoco, his anonymous partner, had won the game. Their fifth win for the night.

He wished he could have watched the emotions play across his brash and ballsy partner's face during the game. But she didn't have a face cam, and she had altered her voice to Darth Vader's bass. He could hack into her system and find her IP address, but it would take a lot of effort. And since she was savvy, she most likely had hidden her identity. Her address had jumped all over servers before landing in a pirate site in Macau or some other untraceable place. And there was the little problem that it was illegal to track her…and what would he do with the information? Call her for a meet-up? Talk about creepy stalker stuff.

But he couldn't help how he felt. They had a connection—how she had anticipated his moves and protected him. They had moved perfectly in sync. The way his life had been going lately, it would be his luck that XChoco was an eleven-year-old boy. But "X" usually meant a female, and his guess was that "Choco" represented a love of chocolate.

Charlie would be laughing his ass right now if he knew how pathetic it was that Reeves, one of the game developers of *Snakes Ahead*, was hoping to get laid by an anonymous gamer because of her quick thinking and her choice of weapons. How sick was that? Reeves would have to agree with his dead friend.

Reeves glanced at his screen. 9:00 p.m. He had been playing for over three hours. He probably should head home. He hadn't wanted to spend much time in the condo. The space felt empty, and the silence taunted him.

He shut down his system when he heard the sound of women's laughter in the high-level security space. Very few had clearance to enter Jenkins Security.

"Sherlock Holmes much?"

Shit, shit, shit. Danni Knorr. He had been good at dodging her until now.

"I wouldn't say it took much brain power."

Yep, Sophie Dean, Danni's bestie too. All he needed was Jordan Dean, Sophie's older sister, to make the holy trinity of interfering women. Thank God, his sister Emily, a professional cellist, was touring on the East Coast.

He stood and prepared himself for the onslaught of female cross-examination.

Danni, as always, was striking in high heels, a tiny skirt, and long, blonde-white hair swaying around her shoulders. The Scandinavian beauty towered over the shorter but no less gorgeous Sophie Dean, who was also dressed for clubbing. The two women loved their dance time. He often had been dragged along with the ladies before they decided that the Jenkins brothers were more interesting.

"God, he looks worse than I expected." Danni marched to him, getting nice and close to his face.

And then she shoved hard against his chest, almost knocking him off his feet. The woman had been working out. "You big jerk. I'm going to kick your ass, and then Sophie…" Danni turned toward Sophie, whose pitiful look was worse than a shove and much more painful.

"What are you planning to do to this big lump of stupid testosterone, Soph?"

"I only have SEAL brotherhood threats from Finn, and all of them sounded pretty awful since they involved Reeves's manly parts."

Danni snorted, then wrapped him in her arms, pulling him close. "Why didn't you tell me? Any of us?"

A lump of emotion stuck in his throat, turning his voice rough. "Not much to tell."

"OMG. Spare me from stupid men." She stepped back and inspected his face. "Not much to tell? Lily was cheating, and you didn't mention it to any of us."

"I spoke with Emily, and you haven't told her either. Why?" Sophie's bewildered voice made him feel like a piece of... Just because he had listened to their heartbreaks didn't mean he wanted to share his.

"What did you expect? That I'd meet for a glass of bubbly and 'process' my feelings?"

Danni's scrutiny was what he had been avoiding. A ferocious and loving woman, she didn't hesitate to get right into any of her friend's business. Thank God Lars was responsible for the woman now.

"You must be really hurting to be such a fricking jerk."

He wasn't in pain, more like regret. He and Lily had started fizzling out at least a year ago. He was more ashamed that he hadn't been paying enough attention to suspect she had another bedmate. How could someone with his IQ be that dense and that trusting? He had assumed that Lily was like his sister and his women friends, who were honest and loyal. Obviously not Lily. Who got their jollies on playing two men? Why couldn't she have broken up with him instead of hiding the truth?

He looked at both women who were like sisters to him. He didn't want them to worry about him.

"Hey, sorry." He shrugged, knowing he failed to fool these women. "How did Finn and Lars let you out of their sight dressed like you're ready to 'partay?'"

"Nice deflection, Reeves." Sophie laughed. "As if Finn has anything to say about the way I dress."

"We're taking you out for a glass of bubbly to get the truth. And if you don't share, we'll sic our men on you."

Reeves smiled for the first time in a long while. He'd take his chances with the ladies. Finn was an ex-Navy SEAL—and one of his bosses—while Lars, Finn's younger brother, was still a Recon Marine. They didn't process feelings. They expressed themselves physically. Very physically. Reeves had been witness to many brawls between the Jenkins brothers.

"I can't wait."

Danni and Sophie wouldn't give up. And he was very tired of his own company. And besides, he hadn't eaten dinner. And how would the women react if he told them he was fantasizing about a gamer he had never met? They'd probably call a shrink.

Still, he gave one last look at his Razer Death Adder Elite mouse next to his Corsair K70 RGB colorful keyboard. What would XChoco think if she ever saw his kingdom?

CHAPTER TWO

Darby Wilson jerked the headset off and stood. "Did we get him?"

After three hours of non-stop gaming, she was relieved to move. The intensity of play frazzled her brain. Reeves Hewitt was a skilled gamer and an excellent partner—anticipating and reacting with situational awareness. She walked to the long bank of computers, where the CIA's finest cybercrime analyst shook her head in disbelief. Molly, her blonde hair caught up in a ponytail and giving her the look of a twelve-year-old, shook her head so hard that her tail bobbed.

"Everything is encrypted, then encrypted some more. He wrote his own security program, and it's fantastic."

"I thought if I stayed on long enough, you'd be able to creep into his system."

"Nope. His firewalls are nothing like anything I've ever seen. I tried every angle I could. The guy's a genius."

"We know Reeves Hewitt is a genius…" Molly's admiration irked Darcy. "A genius criminal."

"He has no record of anything illegal except for the hidden off-shore banking account. And technically, it's not illegal."

Darcy hated Molly's voice of reason.

"He's smart enough never to leave a trail if he hacked into a system, right?"

"Sure." Molly bobbed her head.

"Add in the little fact that he designed the video game currently being used to extract money from the United States."

Reeves Hewitt and his Stanford friend were on Darcy's suspect list because the CIA had tracked the assault on the various US embassies to the video game *Snakes Ahead* that the duo had designed while graduate students at Stanford. The game, a takeoff on Indiana Jones, had been used to plant ransomware into the computer systems in the American embassies in Burundi and Malawi. That was the working theory, at least. One of the designers, Charles Poll, had died in a fatal car accident, but Hewitt and his other buddy, Theodore Thompson, were her number one and two suspects. Hewitt held the top slot because of his position in Richard Dean's software company with DOD contracts to exploit easily.

Darcy was focusing on the game developers while the cybercrime unit was trying to find links between the gamers and any anti-American or anti-government posts. The suspects didn't have any direct criminal ties. Hewitt had even passed multiple security checks with the government and with Dean. But it couldn't be a coincidence that a backdoor program in their game was getting access to government secrets.

The hackers demanded millions of dollars not to release embassy files, which they held in "ransom." The files contained the names of employees and confidential informants, along with the CIA's most sensitive information on Russia's plan to influence the weaker governments in East Africa. The embarrassment of the American government being hacked and held hostage was bad enough on the world stage, but gaining US intelligence and their strategic positioning in East Africa was a political nightmare.

Darcy's team suspected that, despite rigorous warnings, junior members of the staff and guards couldn't resist logging into the game on their downtime. And that allowed the hackers—code name TakeBack—to infiltrate the rest of the embassy. The need to keep the hacking a secret, and prevent any copycat hacking, meant this had to be resolved like yesterday.

"Hewitt can't be held accountable for how his game is being used. And we have nothing on him except that questionable account."

"Which is where he's keeping his illegal gains. We don't have anything on him since he's better than any of our experts. Present company excluded since you did find the bank account."

"The man's a ghost. He had no digital footprint. Everything has been erased or redacted. If I didn't know for sure, I'd think he worked for the Company." Molly cranked her head to the right and left as she shook out her wrists.

Darcy owed the plucky woman for putting in the hours to help her build a case against Hewitt. Intrigued by his skill, Molly saw him as a challenge. Darcy just wanted to nail his sorry ass.

"He's the stuff of a Hollywood hero. He's a lot of man candy and a lot of smarts. The picture of him clubbing with Sophie Dean and her friends is hot. And how about my little discovery that he used the money he made from selling apps to pay for his sister's musical training?"

Darcy snorted. "He's too good to be true. That's why he's perfect for it. And with his security clearance, he has access to DOD's files. Maybe he manipulated them to hide his trail."

The only picture that they were able to pull up, besides his driver's license and passport photos, was taken when Sophie Dean was living out her wilder party days. Darcy felt a kinship with Sophie Dean's need to act out after her mother's death. Darcy had left a spate of bad boys in her wake after her dad died. And Reeves Hewitt had "bad boy" written all over his pretty face.

"I'm surprised Richard Dean didn't use his influence to pull this one."

Molly hit the button, and Reeves Hewitt's angular face filled the giant screen. His thick, ebony hair was disheveled, his black eyes staring at Darcy. He could have been an ad for a men's cologne or a Porsche with his arm draped casually around Sophie Dean, his collared shirt open to reveal a hint of his potent virility. How was this guy a computer nerd? There was no question the man oozed sex-on-a-stick with privilege.

Why did she have such a visceral reaction to this one man? She refused to acknowledge the synergy between them during the three-hour gaming marathon. She thought she had finished with the whole love 'em and leave 'em type. He could be best friends with one of her older brothers. And she had seen the trail of heartbreak her brothers left behind. She didn't require overloaded testosterone to make her life exciting. The CIA gave enough of that.

"Dean might control his computer world, but there's no way he can monitor every picture of his daughter and her friends." Molly smirked.

Darcy didn't have access to Molly's file. All Darcy knew was from comments the young hacker made as an aside. Molly had been a foster kid and seemed to have a lot of trust issues around authority figures. The CIA had recruited her to use her skills for the government, not against it. Richard Dean, billionaire software guru, was the ultimate father figure to rail against. Making Molly the perfect partner for pushing the boundaries but not crossing the CIA line with their deep dive into Hewitt.

"Why do such piddly shit when Hewitt could hack into the main frame of the CIA? The dude doesn't need to use his game to install ransomware. And why countries that are barely on the international radar?"

Darcy hated to admit that Molly's logic was sound. She was frustrated and under a lot of pressure after being sent back to Langley before her fieldwork had been finished. She needed a win, or she would end up behind a desk forever instead of fighting the bad guys. The only reason she had gotten this assignment was that she had been a big gamer before she straightened up her life and joined the military. Instead of attending her college classes, she spent hours gaming, hooking up, and smoking weed.

Wishing Hewitt to be a terrorist didn't make it so. Hewitt was probably too smart to be the perpetrator of the cyberattack. Neither he or Thompson were capable of selling the virus-infected variation to the highest bidder. She had the requisite amount of cyber skills for this op but nothing like Molly or Hewitt.

She was a field agent…or used to be. Her father always

reminded her that her need to win would come back to bite her in the ass. But she grew up in a household of five men—four older brothers and her father, who cast a long and formidable shadow. She wanted a life of adventure in foreign countries, not to be a housewife like her mother, who'd spent her days cooking and cleaning. She'd died before she ever had a chance to live. And Darcy wasn't going to let that happen to her.

The door opened, and a man in an ill-fitting black jacket waited in the entrance. His sidearm bulged under his Men's Wearhouse polyester suit. "Officer Darcy Wilson?"

"Yes." Darcy's heart raced from the formality of his voice and his military posture.

"The director wants to see you. Now."

"He's in his office?" Her voice quavered. It was midnight.

"Yes. He just arrived and immediately sent for you."

The tingling feeling behind her knees worsened when she heard Molly mumble under her breath, "Oh, shit."

"You should hustle." The man gestured for her to go in front of him.

This wasn't the heart-pounding adventure she wanted when she joined the CIA.

Her heart thrashed in loud thumps against her chest when her escort held the door to the director's office. She walked into the darkened space. Two metal lamps on the giant desk were the only light source. She had never met the director, but Andrew Marwick's reputation was that he was a total ball-breaker who did not tolerate idiots or idiots' mistakes.

"You wish to see me, sir?"

Could she be delusional enough to believe that he had breaking information on the ransomware? She stepped farther into the huge office lined with shelves of leather-bound books and gold-framed pictures of the director hobnobbing with world leaders.

He stood with his back to her, surveying the courtyard below. His silver hair was in sharp contrast to his crisp white shirt. Unlike her jeans and t-shirt, he sported a dark blue, almost black, expensively cut suit as if he had just returned from a late-night meeting.

The power suit accentuated his broad shoulders. By his ramrod posture and his linebacker physique, she would've deduced that he was military, like the past directors. Marwick, the exception, was a career diplomat with years of service in embassies across the globe, including West Africa, and part of the reason she wanted to prove herself with this assignment. Embassies were close to the director's heart, as was human intelligence over unfiltered cyber data.

Marwick's appointment was part of the president's mandate that human intelligence and human relationships remained vital to the security of the United States, despite the growing use of AI to gather data and predict human outcomes. She was thrilled with Marwick's nomination since she was the type of agent he'd value. Or so she hoped.

"Ms. Wilson. You've been with the agency a little more than two years?"

"Yes, sir. I was recruited during my second deployment in Afghanistan."

He hadn't offered a seat, so she remained standing at attention as he sat behind his desk.

"You were an Army intelligence officer? Gathering intel from the local tribes."

"Yes, sir. I have a facility with dialects that helped me to reach out and connect with the women."

Witnessing the Taliban's repression of the Afghan women, who previously had attended university and held high-powered jobs, made Darcy appreciate the freedom American women took for granted. And inspired her to keep fighting for democracy and human rights for all global citizens.

Darcy shifted on her feet, not sure where this was leading. Nowhere good, she thought, since she spotted her file on his desk.

"And you received one of the highest rankings amongst your class at the farm. And here you are back at Langley before finishing your first assignment in Senegal."

Her father's advice echoed in her thoughts about eating crow and admitting your mistakes, but not giving up your opinion, even if you were wiped in the grass.

"I was out of line, sir, but I had to speak my mind. My conscience wouldn't allow me to step back from the intelligence and my trust in my CI."

"And you went against direct orders from Station Chief Anders? And shared your intel with your Army liaison."

"Yes, sir." The burn in her chest moved upward. She was sure unattractive blotches now dotted her fair skin. Red heads definitely didn't have more fun. She could control her heart rate but not the dilation of her blood vessels shooting blood to her face and neck.

"Sit down."

Darcy sat on the edge of the seat. Her back stayed straight, and her senses were on high alert.

"Do you know why I'm at my office at this late hour?"

Marwick had skills in interrogation—gifted in dragging this out, making her squirm. She repressed her need to be a smart-ass and commenting that she expected he would tell her very soon.

"The defense department's director called me this evening, interrupting my keynote speech and my dinner. It seems one of my lowly agents has pissed off Richard Dean, *the* Richard Dean, DOD's biggest contractor for our missile defense system and software security systems. A CIA agent attempted earlier today to hack into his employee's personnel files, and not just any employee, but the one that Dean perceives to be like a son. Is this your work, Wilson?"

Damn. She had no spit in her mouth. Total dry mouth like her days baking under the Afghan sun. And Marwick, known for his smooth ability to charm and gently cajole hostile nations into submission, wasn't wasting his skills on his "lowly agent."

"I've been pursuing all leads, sir, including suspects who have allies in powerful places. Hewitt designed *Snakes Ahead* and has high security clearance, and has a suspicious account in the Cayman Islands."

"Now I know why Anders filed a complaint against you. You don't know when to back down, do you?"

"No, sir. Not when I feel the safety of the citizens of the United States is at risk."

"You might have been correct in Senegal, but you're completely mistaken about Hewitt. You're to make nice to Hewitt, beg his forgiveness, and ask for his help with finding who is behind the attacks on our embassies. The man is a genius."

Molly was bad enough, but now her boss was drinking the Hewitt-is-a-genius Kool-Aid. "But sir, he's not…"

He raised his hands to signal her to desist. "You're to be on a flight to Seattle to grovel at Dean's feet. And I mean grovel. Make this right, or you'll find yourself in the basement, never to see the light of day again. Do I make myself clear?"

"Crystal clear." She couldn't keep the frustration out of her voice. Her boss didn't mention that she had saved hundreds of lives that day by clearing the market before the bomb could explode. All anyone remembered was that she had not followed the chain of command. And she thought coming to the CIA would allow her to use her skills at reading people, anticipating their next moves, predicting their behavior, and not be another cog in the bureaucratic wheel.

"You did good work in Senegal. Anders lacks imagination. He's old-school and didn't know what to do with someone like you. The only reason you're not in the basement right now is that I want officers who have a moral compass. But you need to learn how to negotiate, not break men's balls."

Darcy groaned inwardly. There was no comeback the director would listen to. From all her experience at home and in the field, men didn't negotiate. They gave orders and avoided them when she tried to do the same.

But she kept her professional face on. "Understood, sir." And started planning how she could get Hewitt to confess once she met him…

CHAPTER THREE

Enjoying the dark and chocolatey taste of his espresso, Reeves dodged the tourists hustling down Pike Street to the farmers market. He had overslept. He never overslept. His brain never stopped firing all cylinders most days and many nights. But yesterday was not his usual day—a pedicure, a stay in the presidential suite at the Four Seasons, and an extreme workout with the Jenkins brothers. An exhausting, intense thirty-six hours after Danni and Sophie had taken over his life.

The women had planned his "recovery day" to the last second. How could he say no to all their genuine concern? Besides the fact that the Jenkins brothers would have whooped his ass if he had made "their" women unhappy. Not that he'd ever hurt Danni or Sophie's feelings. Having two younger sisters, he was used to meddling women. And as with his sisters, he took the path of least resistance.

Danni, an expert on heartbreak after her fiancé had abandoned her at the altar, was responsible for the spa day, which featured a pedicure and manicure and endless French champagne. He glanced at his buffed nails. If any of the brothers noticed, he'd never stop getting shit from the Jenkins boys who put a capital *M* in macho.

Sophie took a different approach—first, a shiatsu massage with acupressure, followed by a full-body smudge with sage smoke. Sophie had spent time with several indigenous South American groups and was big into alternative healing methods.

Sophie's "therapy" also mandated no contact with his job and no use of his personal devices, including his phone. Since her father was Reeves's boss, he had an unexpected holiday. He was only allowed the TV remote at the Four Seasons.

When the men had shown up at the bar two nights ago and heard what the ladies were planning, Finn and Lars, with dramatic eye rolls, had announced that all he needed was a workout and some horizontal time with a hot woman. The only problem was the workout with spec forces operators was nothing like what civilians did. And Reeves was more than fit, but he was never so glad for the shiatsu massage after what the Jenkins brothers put him through with their usual PT.

And thank God none of his friends had decided to play matchmaker at the bar when they all had imbibed way too much alcohol. The men were right. He needed a woman and sex. He wasn't into booty calls as he had been in college. And he wasn't ready…for anything else. If only XChoco could be real and hot.

He threw his coffee cup into the trash and reached for his phone when he realized he didn't have it. Sophie promised it would be waiting for him at Dean Security's main office. Richard Dean's assistant had left a message at the Four Seasons that Dean wanted to meet with him this morning.

Reeves entered the black-tinted glass and steel building, nodding to the security guard who allowed him to enter the secure private elevator, which served the top floor and Richard's office. Two men in military uniforms and another in a business suit waited with him for the elevator.

Reeves finger-combed his hair, which he hadn't taken time to brush. He wished he had on his better jeans and a clean t-shirt for today's meeting instead of his worn jeans and old Google shirt, an icon appreciated only by fellow geeks.

He allowed the clients to exit the elevator first when they arrived on the top floor. Richard's assistant greeted the men and led them down the hallway.

Reeves was headed in the opposite direction toward Richard's private office when his boss emerged from his office.

Impeccable in his Italian suit, the genius who changed the interface of software grinned before handing Reeves his phone. "Are you better now that you've been smudged? Or did Sophie have to balance your chakras too?"

Reeves hadn't considered that his boss would be privy to yesterday's activities. God, he hoped Sophie hadn't given him the sordid details of Lily mistakenly sexting Reeves instead of her coworker, which the women had extracted from him after too many scotches. He sure as hell didn't want any pitying looks from the man he respected.

"I was spared the chakra-balancing but nothing else. Thank you for the day off. It really wasn't necessary…"

"Of course, it was necessary. Everyone needs time to get away to gain some perspective on what's important."

Richard Dean, a powerful, driven man, had come full circle and then some after both his daughters had been kidnapped by a Chinese gang interested in his older daughter's genetic research. Richard was still as focused, but he was trying to mend all the hurt he had inflicted as he pushed his company to the top of the global market.

Luckily, Richard didn't specify that perspective was on how a lover you trusted was a two-timing liar. The women's outrage on his behalf had helped him come to grips with how pissed he truly was at Lily for not being straight-up with him. Why couldn't she be honest? It wasn't as if they had committed to a future together. And that was part of the problem. He never thought about a future with her. He was having way too much fun fighting bad guys with the Jenkinses.

"And Sophie would have never allowed me to say no," Richard said.

The men laughed conspiratorially. Both techie nerds had an unspoken bond, appreciating that their skills were in front of a screen and not always the best in deciphering human emotions. Case in point, how Reeves had misfired with Lily.

They walked together toward the main meeting room.

"I saw some military types. Are we meeting with them about the software update?"

"You have someone waiting who you'll find much more interesting than the navy brass. I'll introduce you, but this is your project." Richard grinned widely.

Reeves inspected Richard's face for any hint of the reason for the dramatic change in his demeanor. Richard Dean didn't grin. And this was his second grin. Richard was demanding and direct. Mysterious projects and humor were never involved in his business dealings.

Reeves entered the enormous meeting room of steel, black leather, and walls of glass with a panoramic view of downtown Seattle and Puget Sound. Shockingly for the gray Northwest, it was a clear day, giving a spectacular vista of the majestic snow-capped Olympic Mountains.

A young woman with flaming red curls severely held by a clip at her neck was seated at the conference table. A few errant curls had sprung free and danced around her pixie face. She was dressed in a navy blue business suit with an open-collared white blouse, the buttons tugging across her chest.

Reeves pulled his gaze away from the buttons as she crossed the room to greet him but not before she caught him red-handed—or was it red-eyed since he was caught lingering on her stacked chest?

Richard cleared his throat, but Reeves would have sworn that he heard a snicker. Had Sophie's smudging altered his world somehow? Reeves always treated women professionally and didn't leer. Damn, he had sisters. And suddenly Richard Dean had found a sense of humor?

"Reeves, please meet CIA Officer Darcy Wilson, who has flown on the red-eye from DC to meet with you."

The beauty flushed. Bright crimson blotches appeared on her neck and moved upward, spotting her face, and making her green eyes appear brighter. Freckles were sprinkled across her pert nose. Even with her two-inch heels, the top of her head barely brought her up to his shoulder.

What was his problem? His mind was focused on how well she filled out her tight skirt instead of the "CIA" part of Darcy Wilson and the fact that she had flown to Seattle to see him.

Ms. Wilson hesitated before she offered her hand. "Mr. Hewitt, thank you. I appreciate you meeting with me with little notice."

His hand engulfed hers. Sparks of awareness shot down his spine at her mere touch. Reeves held her hand longer than expected, unable to sever the electrical energy sparking between them. Her eyes shot up to his. She stared at him with a direct openness, almost an intimacy. Heat flooded his body, his mind suspended by the raw and honest connection.

He kept her hand in his as he absorbed the delicate angle of her face, the tiny scar that ran across her eyebrow, and the mole next to her lip begging to be kissed. He was close enough to see amber glimmers in her sea-green eyes.

What had Sophie done to him? He was acting so out of character that it was downright scary.

She pulled her hand away and marched with a ramrod spine to her seat. And shit, shit. He had to look, his eyes disobeying the higher parts of his brain pointing out that his behavior was unprofessional. He repeated, "CIA… CIA" to himself, but, unable to control his lower male self, all he could do was track her sweet ass.

"You're going to be surprised by the reason Ms. Wilson is here."

Reeves pulled his shit together and followed Richard to the table. He seated himself across from her.

"If you're not here about our latest patch to our software…then you're here to recruit me, and your trip was wasted."

Richard chuckled. It was a bit eerie to have his severe boss smiling and laughing like a good ol' boy.

Darcy Wilson stiffened, which was pretty difficult since she already sat at attention. He had enough meetings with the military and spent a lot of time with the oorah Marine Jenkins and associates to recognize the training.

"You used to be military before the CIA?"

Her head snapped up. "What does it matter?"

"Just interested. And since I don't know why you're here…"

She cleared her throat and exhaled loudly enough that he could hear her across the seven-foot table. His boss was all about power statements.

"I've been ordered to ask for your assistance on a matter of national security."

Reeves could barely keep from laughing. By her choice of words and her pinched lips, Darcy Wilson was not happy with her assignment.

"I'm all ears to hear how can I help the CIA and you, Ms. Wilson." Not to be an egotist, but the CIA could benefit from his skills, though he'd never last under all the restrictions and rules. Richard Dean appreciated Reeves's need for independence and gave him a wide berth in how he performed his work.

Her lips pressed tightly together with her lower lip tucked underneath and her pert freckled nose scrunched up in disapproval was endearing. And what was wrong with him that he was captivated by this one woman? She was a CIA officer, and he was focused on her every single movement, the slight changes in her color, every little nuance, like how she kept her plump lips compressed as if she was trying to hold the words in.

"What I'm about to disclose cannot be shared with anyone. Do you understand?"

"I'm sure my security clearance covers whatever secret you're about to reveal."

He liked the way the buttons on her blouse looked as if they might pop when she exhaled in irritation. Why was she so easy to rattle? CIA officers were trained in subterfuge and manipulation. How did she ever function undercover?

"The game that you designed with your college buddies has been used in acts against the government of the United States."

All the air left his lungs in one gigantic swoop as it had yesterday when Lars flipped him flat on his back during their Krav Maga workout.

"Who has done what?"

"We believe that *Snakes Ahead* was used to access the servers of two American embassies seventy-two hours ago. They are now locked, and the hackers demand a ransom to give control over to the embassies. Of course, the US doesn't negotiate with terrorists, but the information they've taken is classified, and it's vital that we find who used the game."

"Was the attack Thanos? It's the latest variant of ransomware in the Middle East and North Africa. Which embassies were attacked? If it's what I suspect, the ransomware will be configured to overwrite the MBR unless they get their money. It would mean the server and all files will be erased, and we'll have no chance to get them back. The ransomware often uses the overwrite of the MBR to display the same ransom message. The bigger issue, though, is that the hackers might have made a mirror site and copied the information."

"Mr. Hewitt, I'm a field agent, not a cybersecurity officer. I've been sent here to gather information about the game developers and who, besides yourself and Theodore Thompson, would be able to reconfigure the game to gain access for the attack."

"Did the ransomware leave a message on how to retrieve the files?"

"I'm not at liberty to share all the details of the attack."

"Overwriting the MBR—the master boot record—is a more destructive approach to ransomware than usual. It would require an incredible effort to recover their files—even if you paid the ransom." By the blank look on her face, he was losing her. He was used to watching people's eyes shutter with his techspeak. When his brain was firing, the words were like an overflow valve to help him process.

"Mr. Hewitt. The CIA has an incredible cyber team who are handling the malware. I need to find who perpetrated the attack, not try to crack the ransomware. How easy would it be to hack into the game to use it for malicious intent?"

"Video games have loads of hackers who want to score higher, so they develop cheat apps. I'd like to believe our game is impenetrable. Despite my confidence in my ability and Tex's and Charlie's, there is a possibility that someone was able to penetrate the firewalls. The probability is very low...very low. But it's been years since I've paid any attention to the game. We hired a management company to oversee the business aspects of the game."

She leaned forward, her forearms on the table, giving Reeves a glimpse of her pale skin in the *V* of her blouse. "But you were playing the game last night."

"And how do you know about my playing?" He mimicked her position. "You and the CIA spying on XChoco and me?"

At least she had the grace to blush. The color quickly moved up her chest to her neck and across her cheekbones. Quite a reaction for an accusation that the CIA received regularly. Unless she was XChoco. It couldn't be possible that this serious woman was the bold and skilled gamer, could it? Her uptight suit and no-nonsense bearing didn't match up with the XChoco who spent three hours gaming. But his gut and other body parts were stirring that this bundle of a tiny woman was the XChoco he had been fantasizing about.

"As you pointed out, there are few people who have the ability to hack your game. You must see that you are a potential suspect as one of the developers of the game. Mr. Dean understands our reasoning."

Reeves jerked his head to look at Richard. Why didn't he trust the way Richard Dean was nodding at Darcy Wilson?

"It was a logical deduction on Ms. Wilson's part to consider you and Thompson as suspects. Who else could get through your firewalls? I'm sure your game design protects players from intrusion. The CIA has to consider the possibility that for the right price, one of you may have sold the game to the highest bidder."

Why was Richard ignoring that the CIA had been trying to hack Reeves? Not that they would have any chance at succeeding. And when did Richard condone spying by the CIA? His software was designed, with the help of Reeves, to stop that exact infringement. They might have government contracts, but it didn't mean that he and Richard supported the disregard of the First Amendment.

"I'm going to leave the two of you to settle this misunderstanding. And of course, Reeves, you must help Ms. Wilson find the real culprit. We don't want to make enemies of the CIA, do we?"

Richard was playing some sort of mastermind game. Reeves wasn't clear what it was yet.

Richard stood and moved toward the door. "I can't let the admiral wait too long. I've been able to convince Ms. Wilson that you didn't sell the game, leaving only Thompson as a potential candidate. And since time is of the essence, I've offered one of my jets. I've directed my assistant to have it ready immediately."

Reeves couldn't care less about the CIA's suspicions about him. They were trained to be suspicious and paranoid. What pissed him off was that spooks like Darcy Wilson would consider the unassuming Theodore Thompson a suspect and had no remorse about spying on him. His work with Richard Dean insulated Reeves, but who would protect Tex—a gentle, brilliant soul who would never hurt anyone? Though from Texas, Theodore was the antithesis of a cowboy. He had never ridden a horse, was in favor of gun control, and was a vegetarian. He and Charlie immediately dubbed him Tex when they met him.

Reeves refused to allow Darcy Wilson to harass Tex. No matter how hot she was in her quirky buttoned-up way and his weird and baffling connection with her as XChoco. His fierce reaction to Darcy Wilson had been a momentary lapse caused by his lack of sex for the last two months or some bizarre reaction to all the sage smoke.

"This is a waste of time. Tex had nothing to do with this. You're totally off track. Why don't we Skype with him? And you can head back to DC and trample on other innocent citizens."

Come off like a jackass much? But he had to admire the way Darcy took the hit right on the chin without flinching.

"You've recently been in contact with Mr. Thompson? All we have is his old address in Santa Barbara from a few years ago. And I find it interesting that neither of you has an online presence. Not many individuals can claim that distinction."

"I'm sure CIA officers can claim that distinction. What about you, Ms. Wilson? When I do my deep dive, what am I going to learn? You love cats? Pole dancing?" He was usually a well-mannered polite person, but this woman incited an intense need to poke at her uptight, self-righteous attitude. "And anyone working in the intelligence community or doing highly classified work for the government probably doesn't have TikTok accounts."

"Unless Mr. Thompson is deep undercover with a government agency, which is very unlikely, he remains a suspect."

Reeves had to stop himself from tearing into her. She was doing her job, but she was so off base about Tex. The guy was an introvert and very uncomfortable with people. He was also paranoid about the internet. Anyone with his skills would be. Theodore Thompson wouldn't sell out his country. He had no need. The game had netted fortunes for all of them.

"I haven't talked to Tex in years. He went to Berkeley for his Ph.D. And I stayed at Stanford for my graduate work. He's not a social kind of guy, but it doesn't make him a terrorist."

"You don't have a more recent address? Any way to contact him?"

"No, but I will go with you. I'll need to stop by our security offices before we head out. Don't worry, I'll figure this out, and then you can go back to DC."

He'd find who had hacked their game, protect Tex, and send Ms. Pert-and-Sexy Darcy Wilson packing.

Even if he wondered what it might be like to keep her—just for a while. Sophie and Danni both had suggested a meaningless fling, after all…

Hot, grinding sex with a CIA agent. The sage smoke must have altered his brain since he was liking the idea more and more.

CHAPTER FOUR

Darcy handed her carry-on to the town car driver waiting for them at the Santa Barbara airport. Travel arranged by Richard Dean was a lot more efficient and a whole lot nicer than by the CIA. She had slept the entire flight to Santa Barbara, missing the opportunity to get into Reeves Hewitt's head.

She had dozed off briefly in economy class on the flight out to Seattle. Primarily because of how worried she was about playing nice with Richard Dean, who had the power to send her forever to the CIA's basement. The billionaire had initially been hostile and protective of his "like a son" employee. After hearing her rehearsed explanation and her profuse apologies, Dean had done a one-eighty. He laughed when she divulged that she had spent three hours gaming as Hewitt's partner to hack into his system.

Reeves had given no hint that he knew that she was XChoco. And she hated to admit that she was disappointed that he hadn't acknowledged her skills. And what the hell was that about? She had nothing to prove to the man, a man who was still a suspect. No matter what her boss or Richard Dean said. Since when had the CIA started taking the word of prominent people over the findings from solid investigative work?

Reeves opened the door to the sleek black vehicle and waited for her to climb in. He had been very gentle waking her before they landed. God, she hoped that she hadn't snored with her mouth wide open. With her face smashed against the leather seat, she had dislodged her hair clip and had imprints from the seat on her face. Her hair was now a tangled mess, her curls out of control, and her wrinkle-free suit was failing its promise. The few minutes in the jet's bathroom had done nothing to restrain her wild hair or restore her professional image.

"Were you able to find a current address for your friend?" She craned her neck to look at him. She hated being height-challenged. Damn her brothers for stealing their father's tall genes, leaving her with her mother's short stature, curvy shape, and curly red hair. Her brothers loved to tease her about her unruly hair, calling her "little orphan Annie" or "Carrottop."

"Nothing but the Santa Barbara address."

She smiled at the grumpiness in his voice because he hadn't been able to outdo the CIA and find more info about his friend. She could be generous in victory. Darcy had assumed that while she slept, instead of doing her job getting close to the suspect, Reeves had done a deep dive into her life and his friend. He definitely had unearthed the information about her father's death. It was public record. She would throat punch him if he gave her any sympathetic words or pitying looks.

She scooted across the leather seats, not missing how Reeves watched the way her straight skirt rode up higher onto her thighs. Heat flashed through her body, and it wasn't due to the balmy California weather. She pulled down her skirt and moved closer to the door despite the generous size of the luxury vehicle.

She was used to men checking her out, staring at her chest. She had learned that it wasn't personal but rather part of male hardwiring. The lowest part of the brain shaped their behavior. Listening to her brothers discuss women over the years had helped her not knee every male who eyed her body.

But Reeves's intense inspection had been different—way different. She wasn't disgusted but mystified that she, an ex-soldier devoted to catching bad guys, had captured his interest. He hung out with rich, beautiful women. It went back to that hardwiring thing. Men had to look. But Reeves was so unlike any of the men she knew and worked with. He didn't puff up to demonstrate how shredded or powerful he was or do any posturing as she was used to from her time in the Army. He exuded sexiness without strutting like a damn rooster. He was confident and laid back and still all male and interested in her. And this was a man who hung out with Sophie Dean and her friends.

"Do I need to share the address with our driver?" Darcy had Thompson's address in her Google Maps.

"No, I sent full details to him during the flight. It will take us about twenty minutes to get into the foothills. I'm not surprised that Tex picked an isolated area."

"Is Thompson going to be happy to see you, or should I get my gun out?"

"I didn't think CIA officers carried weapons. Especially on American soil. Isn't your job limited to gathering intelligence… without force?"

"I was joking. But really, is your relationship with Thompson amicable? When is the last time you saw him?"

"Totally amicable. And the last time was at Charlie's funeral. That was almost ten years ago."

He ran his hand through his inky-black hair. His sculpted bicep flexed under his tight Google t-shirt. For a techie, Reeves Hewitt worked out. His ratty white t-shirt didn't hide his six-pack.

Maybe she had to rethink her theory about men's brain capacity. Maybe women behaved no different when it came to certain men.

"We were so young and flying high on the money we had made with the sale of our game. Our timing in the video game market was perfect. Charlie dropped out of school, traveled…and then it all fell apart…"

Darcy understood too well how life changed in a heartbeat, never to return to your carefree self. How your entire world rearranged in a moment.

"That's rough. You and Thompson didn't stay in touch? You didn't get closer because of your mutual loss?"

He twisted to face her, shifting his broad shoulders to loom over her in an attempt to intimidate. She leaned back against the leather seat, away from the glare skewering her.

"Don't use your CIA bullshit techniques on me. It was too painful to be around each other. No scheming for world domination with our game."

"I'm sorry. I'm flying blind here about Theodore Thompson. I'm trying to get a take on your relationship for insight into him. Nothing more."

"Sure. And I have a nice bridge to sell you." He fell back against the seat, looking straight ahead. "Tex is brilliant but shy. The kid who never fit in. He has no need to sell the game to terrorists. No reason. No psychological bullshit will give you a motive for Tex…or me. I'm here to protect Tex, not assist you in profiling my friend into a terrorist so you can move up the CIA's food chain."

"Well, that was clear. And if your friend is innocent, why so much anger on his behalf?" She glared back.

She had a glimmer of respect for Reeves. No one ever called her out except for her oldest brother, who was more like a father to her after her father's death. Reeves wasn't in the least intimidated by her CIA status. Of course not. He had Richard Dean as his ally.

He shook his head. "Don't you ever give up?"

"Not when terrorists are holding our country at ransom. And I'm sorry if I've hurt your sensibilities. But honestly, your feelings mean shit to me. I'm here to do my job."

"Well, that was clear." Throwing her words back at her, he turned and stared out his window. "Once you 'interview' Tex, you can go on your merry terrorist hunt back to DC."

"You don't care that your game is being used against our country?"

"Of course, I do. And I plan to stay and work with Tex and solve how they hacked our firewalls. The company that manages the game does some refreshing of the app. They don't tinker with the source code. It was part of our agreement when we hired them. Have you looked into the employees at our management company?"

She controlled her urge to tell him that she didn't need help doing her job. "Yes. So far, everyone looks clear."

"If there is anyone who can break the ransomware, it will be Tex and me."

She wanted to rail against the man and call him out for his arrogant response, but how could she fault him? She and the CIA needed all the help they could get in solving this fast. And she'd be a fool to turn down his assistance, not to mention her boss's directive. She'd be watching him closely. She wasn't ready to give him a pass…yet. But it was getting more difficult to mistrust a man who wanted to protect his shy friend and save the US. And who made her dormant girly parts wake up and pay attention.

They drove the rest of the way in uncomfortable silence. If she were a different sort of woman, she would try to smooth over the hostility bouncing between them. Women were supposedly peacemakers, but not in her family where it was every man and woman for themselves. The loser got stomped all over if they didn't know how to fight back. She was well prepared for the CIA since she knew when to negotiate and when to do some stomping of her own.

She had to find a connection with these two men and the use of their game. She didn't believe the criminals picked a random game. If Reeves and Thompson were innocent, someone might have wanted revenge.

"Was there anyone else who worked on the game…like a professor or other students?"

She might not be glamorous like the women Reeves was used to, but she was good at her job. She was a damn good agent. And her gut was shouting to keep pushing these men. Tex and Reeves might not be behind the attack, but they were key to finding whoever was.

"No. We developed the game together. It started as a joke, and we were pretty bored with our classes. And writing the game was way more fun and more of a challenge than any of the assignments our professors could come up with. One professor took an interest in our game, but he was interested in all our work since we ended up in his department."

The car climbed into the hills, up a twisting road with

vineyards on each side. She had never been to this area of the country. She knew from the grocery store tabloids that movie stars had homes here, and now she understood why. The day was clear, the sky an azure blue with a few puffy clouds as if arranged in a Monet landscape painting. And the temperature was perfect, warm with no hint of DC's unbearable humidity.

The driver turned into an unmarked driveway. She strained to see over the seat to scout out their approach to the house. The dirt road weaved through trees and bushes as they continued to ascend. Her instincts flared. They were driving into an isolated area. Was this a trap set by Thompson or whoever was behind the attack? It would be easy with Thompson's skill to use the address to lure them into an ambush. At this moment, she wished she had her Sig Sauer tucked into her skirt.

As the car scaled the hilly incline, they finally came into a clearing with the house in view. Three police cars and an ambulance and van with a medical examiner surrounded the ranch-style mansion.

She felt Reeves's body tighten and his inhaled breath. "What the fuck?"

"Let's not jump to conclusions." What an inane thing to say with the ME's van parked front and center. She hated what was coming next for him. In ten seconds, she had made a lot of deductions, and none of them bode well for Theodore Thompson or his protective friend.

Reeves was already opening his door before the driver had stopped.

"Reeves, wait. They're not going to allow you anywhere near…the crime scene."

He strode off, not heeding anything she said. How did she miss that he had a gun tucked into the back of his jeans? What the hell? He wasn't armed when they were on the plane. He must have armed himself when they deplaned. And why was he expecting trouble?

She sprinted after him in her high heels on the gravel. Damn her short legs. Damn her need to impress Richard Dean with her professionalism. With the thirty seconds head start, Reeves was already toe-to-toe with a police officer who didn't look like any of the men who served under her father. The navy-blue short sleeves of his uniform showed his well-formed biceps and his tan skin. With non-regulation long, blond hair, he looked more like a surfer than a uniform who ate donuts as daily sustenance. His posture was relaxed and non-confrontational in the face of Reeves's aggression. No need for a display of power or good ole boy swagger or pushing back by the surfer dude.

"I need to get into the house. He's my friend, damn it."

"Officer…" Darcy paused to read the policeman's badge, "Green." She flashed her CIA badge. "I'm Officer Darcy Wilson. I apologize for my colleague. This is the last known address of his friend and a suspect in our investigation. Can you tell us what happened?"

Officer Green whistled. "CIA? Wasn't expecting that. Does this mean the FBI is going to show up soon too? Should have known. This has professional hit written all over it."

"What the fuck? What happened to Tex? Is he dead?" Reeves's voice cracked.

"There is a thirty to forty-year-old white male with a GSW to his head. We haven't identified the body yet."

"I can identify him. Let me in to see him."

"His face is pretty messed up. It looks as if he was tortured. And the place was tossed."

Reeves bristled, his muscles bunching and his eyes turning steely—all signs of male violence about to erupt.

"Do you have a time of death yet?" Darcy asked.

It was very convenient for someone to have Thompson out of the picture. Did Reeves alert someone to get rid of Thompson and the evidence before she arrived? She had to search Reeves's computer. God, she could imagine what the director would do if she tried to get a warrant for Reeves's computer.

"No, I didn't order a hit on him." Reeves loomed over her, all his hostility now focused on her.

His aggression hit her smack in the solar plexus. He was

hurting, and she should know by now how men reacted when in pain.

"Officer Green, can you give us a minute, please?" Grinding her teeth together, she smiled pleasantly at the local cop who took the hint and walked off to speak to another officer.

She grabbed Reeves's arm and pulled him to face her. "What the hell? Why would you say such a thing in front of the police? You're making yourself look like a suspect."

"You still aren't convinced that I'm not. What difference does it make if Officer Stud thinks so too?"

"Because he's an officer of the law. And despite his hot surfer vibe, he's paying very close attention to you." She squeezed her hands together instead of poking him in the chest. "You're so smug because you have Dean behind you. And you have no idea what I'm thinking. It's my job to investigate everyone."

"Go ahead. Waste your time fabricating theories about me. But if you could get past your damn mistrustful attitude, we could work together. We're in sync, XChoco. Surfer Dude isn't the only one paying attention to you. Your tell is easy. You fold your lower lip under your top one, and you bring your hands together."

The breath deflated in her lungs like a flat tire. She had no comeback. All because of this one man who admitted to paying attention to her. Her usual orderly approach to a crime scene was deteriorating right before her eyes.

"Look. It isn't necessary for you to go in there. The police can run his prints."

"Are you kidding? He was my friend, and I'm going to find the fuckers who did this."

"Keep your voice down. First, implying you might have ordered the hit and then making threats in front of the police isn't helping anything. And you're going to explain to me why you're armed. But not right now. You need to pull it together, or Officer Green isn't going to believe you're with the CIA."

"Don't treat me like I can't handle shit. Tex is my friend…" The strong muscles in his throat worked. "Was my friend."

"I get it. I really do. But there is nothing to be gained from seeing your friend. And you can never take back the image. You don't want to remember him this way. Trust me. It will haunt you for the rest of your life."

Damn his perceptive gaze. He knew she was speaking from experience. She still woke up some nights with the newspaper images of her father, gunned down in the center of their small town.

"You realize the longer we're out here debating this, the local police could be taking Tex's computer, his phone, gaming devices into custody—everything that may help us—or doing who the hell knows what."

"I have jurisdiction here. No one is confiscating anything without my permission. And don't try to change the subject."

He lowered his voice. "I'm no damn ghoul. I don't want to see Tex, but I might be able to detect anything that is off. I knew him."

Why was she trying to protect him? He was a grown man who could handle this in any way he chose.

"Okay. But I swear if you go off or make any threatening comments, I'll have Officer Green arrest you."

"You like making threats." He invaded her space. "You want me in cuffs to have your nasty way? You need to work on your control issues."

She rolled her eyes. Spare her from arrogant men.

CHAPTER FIVE

Reeves would have nightmares for years to come. Tex's face contorted into a barely recognizable bloody, bloated mess; his body in an unnatural position; a gaping hole in the middle of his forehead. Rage and horror simmered close to the surface. He considered every uncivilized thing he'd inflict on the bastards.

He didn't tell Darcy he was leaving. She was fine on her own. Stud Green could give her a ride back to town. The Santa Barbara policeman could ride her every which way to Sunday. He didn't give a damn. Fuck his fantasies that he had spun while she slept on the flight. All centered around her wanton and sexy mass of silky hair—his fingers entangled in all those red curls, making her cry out his name.

Miss CIA found Tex guilty without even meeting him. Any warm feelings for her evaporated the moment Reeves heard her on the phone to the other CIA drones discussing how to get their team out to do the autopsy.

He was finished with the CIA and Miss Darcy Wilson. He'd hack into the CIA if he needed any information that he couldn't glean on his own. His skills might be cyber investigation, but he worked with the best. And his team would find who had tortured and murdered an introverted and innocent man.

Darcy was right about one thing: Reeves could never go back. His worldview had been altered forever when Jordan, Sophie, and Danni had been kidnapped and when the Serbian mafia had come after his sister. Violence was sometimes the only answer.

As he walked to the waiting car, Reeves's phone rang.

"Hey, asshole, not the time to talk. I'll call you in an hour." He clicked off. He didn't care that Nick Jenkins was his future brother-in-law. He was headed to the beach for some time to regroup and think. After listening to the Pacific Ocean with the warm sun on his face and the sea breeze cooling his hot blood, he'd sort out his next move.

Right as Nick called him again, he heard Darcy yelling at him, "Where the hell are you going?"

Her anger was fuel for the fire. This was going to be exactly what he needed. And punctilious, pert Darcy Wilson had a bullseye right on her chest. And then he couldn't look away as her heavy breasts jiggled while she ran in her high heels.

He strode to her, wanting the showdown.

"You bastard, you were going to leave."

"I'm sure Stud Green will take care of you."

"What are you implying?"

He'd give it to her that Darcy was no pushover. She got right up close, not intimidated by the rage roaring off of him.

"Nothing." He shrugged. "You're CIA. You have resources to make your way home."

"I'm sorry about your friend. It was awful for you to see him like that."

"Do you even care that you suspected a good man?" He couldn't stop himself from being a total douche. "All you care about is getting your next promotion."

"Listen, buddy." She poked her puny finger into his chest. "My job is to save lives…as many lives as possible. I get how angry you are that you couldn't prevent Tex's death. I am too. But do you think Tex would hold it against me for trying to find out who hacked your game and made him a possible suspect? Would he have wanted to stop the potential murder of CIA agents and their confidential informants? I think he'd be damn glad to talk with me if he's the man you believe him to have been."

She had been clinical and detached while Reeves had trouble not losing his cookies as she and Green went over the details of

Tex's murder. "I heard you on the phone. Not caring about contacting his parents or his brother, only about his autopsy."

"I didn't think you'd want to be the one since you haven't been in contact with Tex in years. And if a CIA officer called them, it would raise a lot of questions. And the family doesn't need the added stress. The local police will contact his family, as it should be."

So maybe she wasn't a completely insensitive automaton.

She looked behind her and then lowered her voice. "If this is a professional hit, I don't trust anyone but the CIA with Dex's body. Organized crime has its finger in police departments. We might be able to find trace DNA connecting to the men who hurt him."

She was suspicious that the Santa Barbara police were involved? He was a jumble of feelings and not firing in his usual way. Or maybe he wasn't paranoid enough.

"I'm sorry. I can't treat this…" He waved his hand toward the house. "I'm not thinking straight."

"Of course not. I would think something was wrong if you weren't upset and royally pissed. I know you don't believe me, but I'm sorry."

She patted his arm. The heat of her skin next to his warmed the chill that had seeped into him from the blank stare in Tex's eyes, forever imprinted on his brain.

"Hey, don't go there." She hadn't moved her hand, as if she knew she was helping him find his way back from the darkness, bringing him back to the present.

He stared at her tiny, pale hand as she gently rubbed his arm. The sunlight captured glimmers of fire and gold hues in her hair.

"I've been here. And although it's hard to hear, if you didn't have all the conflicting feelings tearing you up, there'd be something damn wrong with you. It's because you're a fine man that this hurts so badly."

He was lost for words, which rarely happened for him. "Does this mean I'm not a suspect any longer?" His joke fell flat.

"No, you couldn't possibly have killed Tex."

"Thanks for the confidence."

His phone beeped. He glanced at the screen, expecting it was Nick harassing him. He had a message on his WhatsApp. He opened the app and read the encrypted one-line message. *Look into Charlie's death.* Followed by a map of Texas.

Reeves stared at his phone. Tex had sent him a message… except he was dead. Reeves had seen his motionless body, the hole in his forehead. Tex must have known there was a chance he would be killed and scheduled the message. Reeves reread the words. Charlie's death was tied to Tex's.

Reeves handed Darcy his phone. "Read this."

"What the hell?" Darcy reread the message as he had done. "Can you find out when he set up the message? Could it have been on a delay?"

"I might be able to get into Tex's WhatsApp account, but it will be difficult. Tex will have set up a lot of firewalls, and he chose WhatsApp to communicate since their encryption is almost impossible to hack."

"We need to find out more. Could Charlie's supposedly accidental death ten years ago be tied to Tex's?" Darcy's phone beeped. "I've got to take this. Don't get any ideas of running off. You need to stay close."

"And if I don't? You gonna use those handcuffs on me?" He invaded her space, moving close enough to see the sunlight reflecting on the amber hues in her eyes. "If you ask real nice, I might let you…"

She rolled her eyes before striding off.

He tracked her round hips swaying and the way she stiffened before she answered her phone.

"Sir?"

Not his usual style of foreplay, but he had a lot of reactions jamming him up, especially around Darcy Wilson. He couldn't resist pushing this woman, a CIA officer who believed in the chain of command and liked order and control. They were direct opposites, but he couldn't stop poking—anticipating her outrage, watching the flush across the delicate skin of her collarbone and her graceful neck. The need to bring that rise of color to her chest and face in a much more mutual and pleasurable way was becoming a persistent fantasy. Darcy wasn't quite ready to acknowledge where the teasing was leading. Not yet. He was ready, had been since he walked into Richard's office and then realized she was XChoco. He knew how he wanted to forget Lily. Forget the mess he was in with Tex. A short, passionate hook-up would make him feel again. And then she'd be gone. No strings, no regrets.

She was shaking her head vehemently to whatever her boss was saying. With her back to him, he couldn't see, but he'd bet that her lower lip was tucked in as she tried to withhold her opinion. This woman did have a problem with authority, or perhaps men in general.

The newspaper article about her father's murder said that Otisville's deputy sheriff left behind his four sons and a sixteen-year-old daughter. Four brothers would give anyone a skewed, or possibly a realistic, view of men's shortcomings. The Jenkins brothers were a perfect example. Despite her tough-guy attitude, she had been gentle and compassionate about Tex. Her body wasn't tough guy. Those soft curves were all woman and hot as hell.

She had tried to spare him from going into the house. But he owed it to Tex, and now to his memory, to find the bastards who were exploiting their game. He needed to get his head screwed on straight and find the a-holes who had hurt his friend. The fight had become real personal.

His phone buzzed. "What's your problem, man?"

"I'm not the one with the problem, asshole," Nick growled. "You're the one in deep shit."

Reeves laughed. Yeah, there was a big difference between the CIA work environment and Jenkins Security.

"You have to tell Emily that you're in danger." Nick was in his Marine Captain command mode.

"Damn it. Darcy shouldn't have called Richard. You know, since the kidnapping, he is very paranoid. There is a risk but not enough to warrant this phone call. Darcy and I have to figure out what Tex was into before buying into a full conspiracy theory."

"Darcy didn't call Richard. The CIA director did. And it's now full-court press on protection detail. No way you're escaping us close and personal."

"Very generous of you to offer, but I'm declining."

"What part don't you get? You have no choice. It sucks what happened to your friend, but you need to talk to Emily." Nick's deep bass made everything he said sound like a threat.

This was all Reeves's fault. He had sent Nick to protect his sister when her life had been threatened. Now he had to deal with Nick in the middle of his family business.

"There is no need for her to know. You know how much pressure she puts on herself during these tours."

Darcy had ended her call and walked toward him.

"Oh, sure. You might get away with that kind of shit with a sister. But there is no way in hell that Emily doesn't expect full disclosure from me about her brother's safety. She'll kick both our asses if we don't tell her."

"Man, take a breath. I'll reassure her that it's all been exaggerated. Or she'll want to cancel her performances."

"I'll convince her not to."

"Good luck with that. You know how stubborn she can be. And if she decides I'm in any danger, she'll want to come back to Seattle. And I don't want her to give up the tour."

"Once I tell her that you have the Jenkins brothers protecting you twenty-four-seven, she'll be fine. She has total faith in my abilities."

"What the fuck? What part do *you* not get? I don't need you guys. I've got my own CIA agent." Reeves waggled his eyebrows at Darcy, who was pretending to be busy on her phone but was tracking every word he uttered.

"Yeah, and I hear that you want her all to yourself. According to Richard, you were struck speechless. Now that I would enjoy. You—unable to talk."

There was no way that Richard had said anything to Nick. He was trolling. God, he hated working with everyone trained in intelligence.

"Shut up, or I'll have to kick your ass." Reeves enjoyed threatening the Marine Raider when there was not a chance that he could take him. Reeves had always trained to remain fit, and after his sister had been threatened, he had upped his game, increasing his stamina and strength and improving his shooting skills. But he'd never catch up with the Jenkinses, all Spec Forces guys with world-class training and years of experience in battle. But none of the guys were master of his cyberworld.

"I'd like to see you try."

"Imagine what Emily would say if you hurt me. I'm her favorite brother."

"Are you talking to the head of Jenkins Security?" Darcy interrupted.

"Yep. And he's acting like an old lady." Reeves hadn't moved the phone to make sure Nick heard.

"I need to speak with him." Darcy opened her hand, expecting him to hand over his phone.

"And why would you need that, sweetheart?"

"Damn it, don't call me sweetheart, and stop being an ass." Her cheeks pinked.

Nick's laughter was loud enough for Darcy to hear. "Oh, I already like her. Let me talk with the officer, douchebag."

Reeves hit speaker and handed Darcy his phone.

"Mr. Jenkins, I've just gotten off the phone with Director Marwick. He has spoken with Mr. Dean about the potential threat against Mr. Hewitt. I'm to coordinate with you on a protection plan to ensure Mr. Hewitt's safety."

"What the hell? I'm not going into a safe house." God, it was bad enough to have his world spinning out of control with the ransomware and now Tex's murder and possibly Charlie's. The last thing he needed was to have everyone hovering around him.

"No one is saying that you need to go into a safe house…yet. As I was saying, Mr. Jenkins, at this point, I don't believe the threat is imminent, but the director would like a backup plan in place if we needed to pivot quickly. You have my full cooperation."

Reeves watched Darcy's lips pucker. He sighed a breath of relief. Darcy didn't want the Jenkins agency involved any more than he did.

She said, "Is there a way that you can procure me a weapon? Reeves, who I assume is licensed, has a Glock, but I'm without a firearm. My flight was last minute, and I couldn't get clearance to bring my weapon on board."

"No problem, Ms. Wilson. Name it, and I can have it to you tomorrow."

"That's impressive. I'm not sure I want to know."

"Nothing illegal. I've arranged for you to spend the night at the home of a friend of Sophie Dean. The actress isn't in residence, but her house is highly secure and has a security team who will be able to procure your firearms."

"I'd like a Sig P226."

"I like a woman who knows what she needs. You have my permission to marry her, Reeves."

"You didn't ask my permission to marry my sister."

Nick barked his amusement. "I informed you of my plans."

"Mr. Jenkins, is it with you that I coordinate Mr. Dean's jet to fly us to Palo Alto in the morning? I need to be on-site here for at least several more hours. Reeves and I will need to check out Tex's last residence and possible connections in Palo Alto. We might have to spend the night there. And it is best to be off the radar with our accommodations."

Reeves didn't miss that Darcy hadn't shared Tex's message about Charlie's death.

"Please call me 'Nick' now that you're going to be in the family."

Darcy rolled her eyes, her only response to men's outrageousness. Probably how she coped with her brothers.

Reeves had a much better way for her to cope. Now, if he could only convince her to participate.

CHAPTER SIX

After their ID check at the front gate, the overbuilt, steroids-shooting guard had escorted Darcy and Reeves to Merissa Storm's estate entrance. Darcy stood next to Reeves in the dramatic wood and slate entrance as Jonathan, the manservant in a fitted black suit and crisp white shirt with his blond hair slicked back, welcomed them. The smell of salty sea air and the crash of the waves in the open-air waterfront villa was surreal and unsettling after the grisly crime scene.

As they all stood in front of the bank of monitors, Reeves grinned from ear to ear like a child on Christmas morning, listening to Jonathan's description of the high-tech surveillance. This was the first genuine smile she had seen on Reeves's face since their arrival in California. And why did she find his absorption in surveillance technology endearing? His crazy mix of alpha male on the prowl and nerdy tech geek made it difficult to reconcile her forceful attraction. Damn him for not fitting into the box she had assigned to him. It was a whole lot easier when he was a suspect.

If she thought there could be anything more between them than a few hookups, this was the moment when the gap in their worlds opened to earthquake proportions. Reeves accepted this outrageous opulence without a blink. Darcy's comparable experience in luxury was a weeklong stay at a Four Seasons in Dubai when she was undercover as a banker to investigate a money-laundering ring.

Otherwise, her only exposure to this level of affluence was from magazines or reality TV shows. It was as crystal clear as the infinity lap pool that there was no future between a cop's daughter and the worldly man with connections to movie stars and billionaires.

Sure, they had chemistry, but chemistry only got you so far. As she had learned at an early age, most men saw her as a target. Her red hair, big boobs, and curvy behind screamed "easy sex" to men, and Reeves was no different. She had seen how he stared at her chest.

She completely checked out once the men became enraptured discussing encryption codes. Instead, she stared at Reeves's profile. Dark stubble covered his strong chin, his hair was disheveled, and his full lips were the color of Afghan pomegranates. Somehow his rumpled look came off sexy instead of a gamer who never left his basement. He had the habit of rubbing his hand through his thick locks when he was engaged.

"I'd like to walk the perimeter." She didn't like entrusting either her or Reeves's safety to strangers who she hadn't vetted or to a surveillance system that could be hacked.

Both men stopped and stared at her as if she had unbuttoned her blouse and exposed herself.

"It isn't necessary. There are surveillance cameras and heat and motion sensors on every inch of the outside grounds." Jonathan's condescension quickly became grating.

"The hundred-foot cliffs are a solid barrier to possible assault by sea."

The ocean side of the villa was all glass except for the supporting beams optimizing the view of the Pacific.

"The windows are specially tinted to prevent the paparazzi from using helicopters to invade Ms. Storm's privacy."

"I'm glad to hear that surveillance is in place, but I never rely solely on tech." She smiled sweetly. She didn't try to act impressed by Jonathan's reassurances and didn't care that she interrupted the men's tech bonding.

"I can disengage the system once Jonathan leaves so you can do your thing." Reeves's eyes lit up with amusement.

Thank God, Reeves was a quick study and only needed a few minutes to master the system; otherwise, she might have hurt Jonathan if he didn't stop talking. All she wanted was to get out of her wrinkled business suit and uncomfortable heels and into her runners and sweats.

"I usually prepare dinner for Ms. Storm and her guests."

"Thank you, Jonathan, but Ms. Wilson is a gourmet cook and likes control of the kitchen. Plus, we've kept you later than usual."

Reeves's face and voice never betrayed his big fat lie. She pressed her lips together to stop herself from laughing. Sure, she was a gourmet chef and a pro-basketball player. During travel, Darcy usually made do with nuts, protein bars, and a dark chocolate bar—or two or three—that she always had packed in her bag.

"I'm that way myself. I hate interruptions when I'm creating."

She nodded at Jonathan, knowing he wouldn't wait for a reply.

"Since you're a chef, you'll appreciate the kitchen."

Reeves subtly widened his eyes. "I'm sure Ms. Wilson will be thrilled to hear about the details of the kitchen. Leave the tech talk to the men. Be warned. Once she gets started on her sauces, it's a real snooze fest."

Reeves Hewitt was a dangerous man. There were loads of men with beautiful faces and bodies but not many with his twisted humor. Not many men could tease her and not get their asses kicked. Instead, she found his devilish grins and absurd comments seductive. She needed some distance. If only she had packed a bathing suit, she'd do laps safely in the water, protected from doing something really stupid.

Reeves, with his bag swung over his shoulder, followed Jonathan into the kitchen.

Reeves slowed his pace. Looking over his shoulder, he whispered conspiratorially out of Jonathan's earshot. "Have you seen any of Merissa Storm's movies?" And then there was the grin that Darcy couldn't look away from. Reeves was a striking man in repose, but his hard angles eased when animated, and his coal-black eyes brightened from an inner fire.

She found herself grinning back, leaning toward him and his diabolical enjoyment. Heat flooded her body, and her breath quickened at his closeness.

Something must have shown in her eyes or in the flush stealing across her chest and neck.

Reeves halted with an arrested look. "I feel the same way." His voice took on a dark, edgy tone.

She was weakening. So what if they had nothing in common? Who cared? She didn't want to marry the guy. She had goals, aspirations, and a lot of adventures ahead. What would be wrong with two consenting adults offering each other comfort after the day they had experienced? And Reeves was the kind of man who would offer her comfort, not just impressive orgasms. He betrayed his kindness in the hours they were together. The way he spoke affectionately about his sister, his emotional reaction to his friend's death, and the gentle way he had woken her on the plane. No one ever treated her carefully or tenderly as if she was important or fragile.

She hadn't had been in a relationship for a while. Now, it was mainly hookups with men like herself who needed to blow off steam from the dangerous work. The CIA pushed relationships amongst their employees. It made keeping your secret life less difficult if your husband was also an officer. She got together with a fellow officer. It lasted for almost four months, her longest relationship, when they were both in DC. Once she got her assignment to Senegal, she ended it. Her career came first.

And there were no rules against fraternizing with Reeves. It wasn't as if he was a suspect.

She'd never admit it, but holding onto the idea that he was a suspect had been a flimsy excuse to protect herself.

Jonathan, ignoring or oblivious to the sexual tension, showed her the induction cooktop, the blender for emulsions, and the liquid nitrogen tank. Who knew that you could cook with liquid nitrogen? The only use she knew was for creating explosions.

She was enjoying giving Reeves death stares every time Jonathan looked away. Her heart fluttered like a teenage girl's at the way Reeves's lips twisted into the smallest smile.

When Jonathan opened the refrigerator and freezer to show them how well-stocked it was, Darcy considered her escape options since she either had to knee Jonathan to shut him up or kiss Reeves. And neither were viable choices. But if she stood any longer in her high heels, she would detonate. As her brothers could attest, it was never a pretty sight when she lost control.

"Since Ms. Storm might decide to fly up from LA on a whim, I have to be prepared."

Reeves's heated glances weren't helping her control. Neither was Jonathan's demonstration of multiple machines to make coffee.

"Thanks, Jonathan. I think we can figure out the basics." Reeves slid his Glock into the kitchen drawer closest to the front door when Jonathan had his back to them. She would have liked to have the handgun in her possession. This was a compromise that she could live with. She didn't have to take his gun since she was confident she'd be quicker in getting to it if she needed it.

"We've had a long day and are ready to crash. What bedrooms are open?"

Darcy's glare should have scorched a burn on Reeves. It was one thing for her to consider tearing his clothes off and running her lips down his sculpted body, but it was another issue, a big fricking issue, for him to assume tonight was a done deal.

"Please give Ms. Wilson an ocean view room. We want her to relax and enjoy the splendor of the Pacific. She's had a trying day."

Shivers of excitement fused with apprehension that he could read her that well. She was the one trained to read people.

"Is there any chance that there are extra bathing suits? I need a workout." Her face burned crimson at her choice of words. "I have a lot of work tonight, and it would be great to swim as a break."

She scowled at Reeves before turning her attention to Jonathan.

Jonathan inspected her with a professional, impersonal air. "Of course. And we have several suits that will fit you. If you give me your suitcase, I'll unpack, turn down the bed, and lay out the suits for you."

Darcy hoped her mouth didn't hang open. She had entered another universe where someone actually unpacked your suitcase. "Thank you, Jonathan, but that won't be necessary."

She wasn't comfortable about anything in this entire situation. Especially not with being stranded in an unplanned location with a man who made her think about sex instead of possible threats and a deadline to find the perpetrators. Where was Darcy Wilson, dedicated CIA officer? Give her a nice terrorist cell to infiltrate, and she was in her element. But a hot dude and a non-stop talking manservant who catered to any of your needs? Now, that was throwing her off her game.

"Ms. Wilson is a very private person." Reeves waggled his heavy brows. "And you never know what you might find in her suitcase."

Jonathan's face hadn't registered any change. He was the classic unflappable butler from old movies.

"Ms. Wilson, if you follow me, I'll show you the bedroom and your choices in suits."

Darcy trekked behind Jonathan, who pulled her carry-on down the open-air hallway. Her heels clicked on the slate floor. The house's grandeur was understated by the natural color of the rock cliffs used throughout to blend with the magnificent setting. The beauty of the Pacific Ocean was center stage. During the day or at sunset, it would be spectacular, but even now, it was impressive.

She felt Reeves's stare on her back. She refused to look over her shoulder and give him the satisfaction of her awareness and anticipation flitting down her spine. She wasn't here on a beach vacation to do the nasty. She was on assignment. What had happened to the highly disciplined woman who always kept her goals in the front view?

Darcy sorted through the three "bathing suits." All were designed for lounging on a chaise sipping exotic fresh fruit drinks, and for quick and easy removal in the heat of the moment. She held up the matching flowered halter and tiny bottoms, which would reveal more than cover. The tiny scraps of material would offer no support while exercising. Who did laps in a thong or pushed the conditioning envelope in a skimpy halter?

Could she give up swimming in the most magnificent pool in the most incredible spot—an experience she'd probably never have again—because she didn't want to give Reeves the wrong impression? She wasn't offering an invitation just because she was attired to hang out at Hugh Hefner's mansion.

Her feminist heart became outraged on behalf of all womankind. No male would need to consider his choice of suits as a ploy. She held up the neon-yellow bikini. The top was smaller than the flowered one if that were possible.

Her choice wasn't about seducing Reeves. She wanted to swim so she wouldn't be tempted to take a tumble with sexiness incarnate in the gigantic bed—convoluted logic, but any woman would understand.

She kicked off her heels and shed her skirt. She was an incredible athlete who prided herself on her strength, stamina, and strong curves. Survival in the Wilson house depended on excelling in everything physical. No one and no bathing suit would interfere with her taking advantage of an amazing lap pool on the edge of a cliff overlooking the Pacific Ocean.

She should strut in the bikini and jump into the pool as a way to say to Reeves, "deal with it." But the problem was she wasn't ready to deal with it—sex with Reeves—molding her lips to his, touching all that man, seeing him naked…and taking the risk.

The path of least resistance was the heavy terry cloth robe hanging behind the bathroom door.

CHAPTER SEVEN

Reeves sat in front of the fire pit, a computer on his lap, shifting his gaze between the moon over the ocean and his screen. The sounds of the waves and his fingertips gliding over the keyboard helped settle his swirling brain. He searched the online newspaper articles on Charlie's death, trying to figure out what had triggered Tex's investigation of the accident. Had Tex believed that Charlie was murdered? And if Charlie had been murdered, why was his death covered up to look like an accident? And did the same person kill Tex? The image of Tex lifeless on the floor was seared into his brain and not going away soon.

He was glad that he had a focus to keep him busy. He wouldn't be getting any sleep in the foreseeable future from the visceral memory of his friend and his very visceral needs for Darcy. Having her nearby and not touching her guaranteed many restless nights ahead. She was slowly becoming a challenge he needed to unravel. As his early delving into Python script, he wanted to peel away every layer of Darcy's protective shell to the soft, vulnerable woman.

When they entered the mansion, she tried to hide her shock, but he felt her every breath as she took in the over-the-top luxury. And her reaction to Jonathan's condescension was as he expected. Darcy didn't suffer fools or pretensions. And he liked her for not being impressed with the manservant role and the blatant wealth and privilege.

He leaned closer to the screen to study the picture of Charlie's red car crashed into a tree that had been published in the *Palo Alto Weekly*. All three of the city's newspapers ran the same picture and the same story. "Rich tech millionaire crashes his Lamborghini. Cocaine found." In Silicon Valley, Charlie's death was but a ripple in the area of extreme excesses. Some of the young millionaires couldn't handle the sudden enormous wealth and got lost along the way. It was what was assumed about Charlie. He was high and lost control of his car.

Reeves felt Darcy's presence before he heard her quiet footsteps moving across the slate. His breath hitched at her nearness. His muscles tightened; his skin prickled with awareness.

She said nothing as she passed him. Placing his laptop on the ottoman, he stood, unable to ignore her.

"The pool is heated, but the air temperature is dropping quickly. It will be chilly when you get out." Smooth, Hewitt. He sounded either like a weatherman or a whiny old man. The need to kiss her, to touch her, had escalated to insane proportions— watching her eyes dance with mischief, her lips compressed to stifle her laughter, her cute death stares as an attempt to discourage his ridiculous comments to Jonathan.

She was wrapped in a thick terry cloth robe, and she had tightly cinched it, emphasizing her small waist and the womanly flare of her hips. Her hair was pulled up in a twist on top of her head, suggesting exploding fireworks, all the fire spilling over and down her face.

"You're going to swim?" Her eyes narrowed as she examined him in the only bathing suit that fit. He was a big man, and it seemed the Hollywood types were short. He tried not to react while her eyes lingered.

"Not a long season to swim outdoors in Seattle." *What the hell? Just shut the fuck up, Hewitt.* Her less than enthusiastic reaction to the idea of him swimming had him spouting drivel to fill in the tension. Her lips pressed together, and her chin thrust forward didn't take his genius IQ to read. Flirty games were done. She was back to being the distant professional.

"I can wait until you're finished if you like. I'm looking over the news clippings of Charlie's accident."

"Did you find anything?" She shifted on her bare feet. He was mesmerized by the delicate arch of her feet and her red-painted toenails. Not as buttoned-up as she wished everyone to think. He bet his little officer liked racy underwear. Not the best to dwell on Darcy in lingerie when wearing nothing but a swimsuit. "Just getting started…but nothing helpful yet."

"Tomorrow, I'd like to stop first at the Palo Alto police station. It's a small station, so we might be able to shake out memories from Charlie's accident. I learned from my dad that impressions don't show up in written reports."

"If I only had Tex's computer or his phone. I could track his searches about Charlie. I'd know what he was looking for. Any news from your tech person?"

"Molly and the team are working on the malware. It's a top priority for the cybercrime unit. But I've another team searching the security cams that Tex had just installed. They're running his credit cards and financials. He was skilled at hiding a lot of his info. They're checking airport manifests to run the passengers through our database for the hired hit since Santa Barbara is a small airport. We might get lucky and find who traveled to do the hit. The town doesn't look as if it has a lot of local paid-for-hire assassins."

"But LA is only a two-hour drive. Safer to fly into LAX and then drive."

"I should text her to look into car rentals from LAX."

"Go swim before the wind starts up." What was wrong with him and his insane comments about the weather? Darcy Wilson was what was wrong with him. Her pale skin was exposed in the *V* of her bathrobe, and despite the thick material of the robe, the outline of her heavy breasts was conspicuous. How easy would it be to untie the robe? Didn't she understand men's minds? It was part of the predator gene to want to claim whatever was hidden.

"I don't care if you want to swim laps too. The pool is big enough for both of us to stay in our lanes."

"I promise not to cross your lane…unless you ask me nicely. Really nicely." He couldn't stop the husky timbre coloring his voice.

Her breath hitched before a Cheshire cat smile lit up her face. "I'll hold you to your promise."

Her exaggerated hip swaying as she sauntered away heated his blood to the boiling point. The woman was up to something. Was she planning on skinny-dipping? The idea had short-circuited his mainframe. He tracked her slow, seductive walk. He'd never be able to keep his promise.

She threw her towel on the chaise lounge, walking to the edge of the pool to dip her foot into the water. His heart, hammering in his chest, reverberated in his ears like a live Radiohead concert. He couldn't look away from the drama of waiting for Darcy to take off her robe. This was better than waiting for Apple to introduce the iPhone.

With her back to him, she leisurely untied her robe and let it drop to the ground. He was paralyzed. Unable to breathe or move from the vision of Darcy in a tiny thong, her heart-shaped ass exposed. Lust, incendiary lust, swamped him as he imagined the ripe globes squeezed between his palms. Never before had a woman struck him so thoroughly, so quickly.

She turned, and he stared, mouth open. His brain and body freeze might be a sign of a stroke. Her beautiful, round breasts were in a skimpy, barely-there halter.

"You remember your promise?" She waggled her eyebrows in imitation of him.

Promise? What was she talking about? His genius brain was like scrambled eggs. He couldn't form a thought or word if he tried. All the blood for his brain had gone south. His body was hot and hard.

"You promised to stay in your lane unless I asked nicely. I'm not asking…but if you beg, maybe just maybe, I'll let you in my lane."

She dove into the pool with perfect grace and didn't emerge until she reached the end of the pool.

He had no pride. He'd beg. He'd grovel. He'd do anything to catch her. And when he did…

He ran to the edge and dove in.

Darcy was a strong swimmer, and she already had finished the lap and was heading toward him. He waited, and when she was in reaching distance, he lunged underneath her. She anticipated his move, turned rapidly, and swam away from him. She had a lot more maneuverability with her tiny frame, but strength and size were on his side. And his drive to capture her.

He grabbed her ankle and hauled her back, watching her fight against his hold. He had to touch her, run his hands over all those soft contours. She twisted underwater and slipped away. Her escape only heightened his arousal to claim her. He picked up his speed, and this time, she wouldn't get away.

So near, he swam past her, staying in his lane. It took all his discipline to stick to his plan when she was within reaching distance. But he was determined to outsmart this very smart woman. He rolled through a flip turn at the end of the pool and swam back toward her. It took every cell of resolve to not touch and do another lap. He wanted her to let down her guard, and then he'd catch her. But when she glided past him, he lost all his resolve; he accelerated, his strong strokes cutting through the water. He grasped her calf, his large hand covering the sleek muscle. He never felt more grateful for his size and strength.

He dragged her toward him. His heart and breath hurtled with his burst of energy as the glistening woman wrestled against his grip. She flipped over and kicked him hard in the chest with her other foot. He tugged her closer, searching her face for clues whether she was still enjoying the game. She had thrown down the gauntlet, and like any breathing male, he took up the challenge. Did she desire the sparring to end the way he did?

Her green eyes brightly glimmered in the moonlight. As he tugged her near, she wrapped her legs around his torso and sat up, connecting them chest to chest. Her muscular legs molded tightly.

The sensation of her full, hot breasts against his chest made his knees almost buckle. His throbbing dick was pressed against her soft mound as his hands caressed her ass. He was building to blow just by groping her sumptuous ass. He dragged himself back from the precipice. He wanted to make this good for her.

He brushed away the lock that covered her one eye—silky as he had imagined. He stared into her eyes. Their jagged breaths mingled, as did their speeding hearts.

"Is this what you want?" He flexed his hips, bringing his dick against her entrance. He was one skimpy layer away from thrusting into her and taking them both to nirvana.

"Believe it or not, I came out to swim, not to seduce you. But you…"

Her long, red-tinged lashes sparkled with water droplets, as did the pale skin of her cleavage. He wanted to lick every drip.

"You…you make me violate all my rules." Her teeth clamped on her plump lower lip.

"I'm so glad to hear that we're in the same place…since I've never had this response to a woman before."

She laughed, her breasts jiggling in the little top that he wanted to rip off. She lifted herself and pushed against his erection. "First time. Now that's just sad at your age."

He roared. The deep laughter filled the empty spaces around his heart with joy. "For that, you're going to pay."

"Bring it on, Hewitt. I can handle anything you have."

She reached down and gripped him hard. He throbbed against her tiny hands. Red sparks shot before his eyes, and pleasure rolled down his spine, straight to his balls. He was going to lose it before he got to taste and enjoy every wet inch of Darcy Wilson.

He moved quickly to shallower water where he could stand, but where they would still be underwater. He was steaming hot, but he didn't want Darcy to get chilled. And treading water was a distraction when he wanted his focus only on the gorgeous woman, a living dream, in his arms.

Resting against the edge of the pool, he couldn't stop squeezing her ass between his palms as he searched under the thong. Darcy gasped and rubbed her chest against him as his long finger stroked along her swollen vulva. He circled her bud, feeling it swell and thicken under his touch.

Aroused, Darcy started to ride him, moving up and down. The friction of her voluptuous breasts against his chest, and her mound against his dick, was pushing him right to the edge. He didn't want a quick fuck for their first time together. He wanted to take her nice and slow and savor what a lucky bastard he was that this smart and sensual woman had come to his bed.

Her face was flushed and her movements more frantic. She was ready to detonate, and he wanted his mouth on her breasts when she did.

She groaned in distress when he stopped touching her to release her halter. He lifted her wet, heavy, and full breasts. His body and his dick got harder and hotter, which seemed impossible. He bent and licked her tight, pale pink nipple. He licked slowly, relishing the taste of Darcy as his fingers explored along her slick folds, avoiding touching her clit. He wanted to enjoy this moment of Darcy, her head thrown back, all fire and passion, floating on sensation.

He switched and licked her other nipple, enjoying her loud groans. She kept moving, her movements more frantic, reaching for her orgasm.

He sucked her breast, pulling as much of the supple tissue as he could into his mouth. He couldn't stop thrusting against her. He couldn't control his need to respond to her gyrations that brought her sweet heat directly against him.

He was edging to his release. He circled her clit in a gentle rhythm, watching Darcy climb, panting, and riding him with abandon. Her sodden hair had partially come undone and hung around her shoulders; her eyes were closed and her mouth open with her tiny gasps. He sucked harder on her nipple and then scraped his teeth across it. She went off, exploding in his arms, screaming his name. He didn't stop his careful worship of her breasts and kept his finger lightly encircling her as the waves subsided.

She collapsed, her head resting on his chest. Her breath still came in short, little puffs. As he soothed her back, a sense of well-being filled him. Giving Darcy orgasms and comforting her felt right—better than solving any algorithm.

He kissed the top of her head as he began to walk toward the steps, desire's pulsating beat drumming through him for the night ahead. The first time might be a little rushed since it had been a long time, but they had the whole night.

Suddenly, an alarm blared through the silence. *Holy shit.*

Darcy stiffened and then catapulted out of his arms onto the pool deck and ran toward the entrance.

She shouted as she ran topless toward the bank of monitors. "Get down and stay down."

Fuck. Fuck. Fuck. He'd set the alarm to signal when anyone approached the front door. The blare was coming from his computer and not the entire system.

He jumped out of the pool and ran after her.

In the seconds ahead of him, she had his Glock out of the drawer in the kitchen where he had placed it and was loading it as she snuck toward the front door.

"Darcy, stop!"

She raised her hand and then whispered without a pause in her prowl, "Get in a room and lock the door. Now."

"I reset the alarm, so if the guard or Jonathan came back, it would alert me. Unless an intruder got past the guard and the surveillance system, it's one of those two."

She halted. Her back to him. Her voice cold and hard. "Repeat that."

"I overrode their passwords so they couldn't get in without me knowing it. I wanted my system in place after what happened with Tex. And I didn't think either of us wanted Jonathan to return."

She swung around, the gun now pointed downward, but the fury on her face and in her eyes made him step back. With her damp red hair curling around her head and her look of murderous rage, she resembled a revenging Valkyrie.

"And you didn't think to tell me?" She punctuated each word. "To keep me in the loop about our security?"

He raised his hands. "It's just habit to reset passwords when any of our clients are in a safe house. Limiting it to only select people knowing the password. It's a safety measure." Surely, she could see the logic. He tried to keep his eyes on her face, but her skin was dewy, her hair starting to curl, brushing her taut pink nipples.

"You answer the door. I'm taking a shower." Her lips compressed into an accusatory and angry line. She marched past him without a glance.

"I'm sorry. I should have told you. I forgot."

"Sure, you did," she said under her breath, making it loud enough to make sure he heard. "Nothing to do with your plan to get naked."

He didn't think she'd appreciate it if he pointed out they hadn't gotten naked yet. He couldn't deny he had hoped for a night with Darcy, but he wasn't devious or desperate enough to have a master plan. But Miss Suspicious would never believe him or the fact that some humans didn't have malicious intentions.

And he was the biggest asshole because, despite his plea that he was as innocent as a choir boy, he turned to watch her fine body in a thong sway down the hall.

Shaking his head, he moved to answer the door after checking the monitors. The security guard was at the front door and was most likely bringing Darcy's Sig.

CHAPTER EIGHT

Darcy held the door for Reeves as they exited the Palo Alto police station. The information from the police chief had not been at all what she had expected. She was having trouble making the three hundred sixty turn on her investigation with all the implications. And if she was having difficulty, Reeves had to be in shock, spinning and confused.

He followed her to their rental SUV and climbed into the passenger seat without a word. A silent Reeves was disturbing. When upset, Reeves reverted to rapid tech talk. On the way to the airport, he had tried to explain the difference between C++ and Java coding and their use in video games. As if she had an interest in the comparison.

He filled in all the tense silence from last night's little swim. He had tried to talk to her through her door after she stomped off. But if she stayed, she might have physically hurt him. She had been totally pissed, feeling as if she had been played. Once the adrenaline surge subsided, she appreciated his logic and pretty quickly let go of her anger toward him. She was still pissed but only at herself for how badly she had messed up.

She needed to clear the air and make sure they returned to a professional relationship before they got in deeper with the investigation. She hated that this trip had become one shock after another for Reeves. He was a good man and didn't deserve to have landed here. The aftermath of a brief hookup felt irrelevant when Reeves had to deal with so much.

"What are the chances that the detective's CI was wrong about Charlie?" He didn't look at her but remained fixed, staring through the front window.

He had dark circles under his eyes, and his beard was already getting stubbly despite shaving this morning. And even drained and exhausted, he still was able to make her stomach flutter. Her resolve to get back to platonic had evaporated the moment he came out of the bedroom for their flight. With his thick hair brushed back, emphasizing his prominent cheekbones, looking incredible in a tailored black suit that showcased his broad shoulders, he looked every inch the wealthy and sophisticated man that he was…and she was neither wealthy nor sophisticated. She sent an imaginary memo to herself. *Not the man for you, no matter how gorgeous and wonderful.*

"Detective Barley was pretty confident that Charlie is alive and working with the Sureños. Do you believe him?"

She wanted him to talk. Let it all out. Nothing about this was easy. She wanted to comfort him, but it would send the wrong message. He was an asset. And she had crossed the line with him. She owed him an apology.

"Detective Barley is solid and seasoned. And his faith in his CI working undercover in the Sureños gang seemed deserved." He shifted in the seat and stretched his long legs. "Does this mean that Tex had learned that Charlie was alive?"

Darcy tracked the way the fabric hugged his lean, muscular thighs.

"It's all too much to take in. Now, Charlie is alive, and Tex is dead. I don't have a clue about what's going on," Reeves said.

She twisted to face him. "You've been hit with a lot in the last twenty-four hours. And we don't have any definitive proof that Charlie's alive. But if Charlie got in too deep with drugs, he might have staged his death to avoid a drug deal gone wrong. He couldn't let whoever was after him find out he was alive."

"Why stage his death if he's working for the drug dealers? The Sureños are a Mexican drug gang that associates with the Sinaloa Cartel. You heard the same explanation from Detective Barley.

His CI reported Charlie because he overheard one of the gang members say the white dude was 'loco' because he wrecked his Lamborghini ride. He sold his tech skills for drugs or money. It must be for drugs. He didn't need money."

"He might have been forced to work for the Sureños to pay off his debt to them. With a drug habit, he could have run through his money. Did he have a drug problem in college?"

"No. But once we got our first big payout, he disappeared. He might have started self-medicating to either belong to the wealthy, cocaine-snorting Silicon Valley crowd or to escape the isolation."

"Isolation?"

"Sure. There aren't many people who can understand the pressures of being 'gifted.' Only others with the same talents, and they aren't always the most socially engaging kind of people. And you know what kids are like if you don't fit in? Adults aren't any different."

She did. But being a genius versus having big breasts didn't seem like a comparable situation.

The only girlfriends she had in school were the ones who wanted to get to her brothers. Girls came over to her house but not because of a desire to be her friend. She was the chubby girl with big breasts who hid under oversized sweaters.

And the boys only saw her for one portion of her anatomy. If she didn't have tough-ass older brothers who protected her and cued her into the score, she might not have survived middle and high school.

Had Reeves been bullied in school? He was so confident. Definitely attractive, he must have had tons of friends. Richard Dean liked and respected him. And so did Sophie Dean. She could see Dean wanting Reeves as his son-in-law even if she was with Finn.

"If Charlie works for the cartel, he could have been the one to engineer the ransomware attack on the embassies. He could easily hack the game's firewalls. But why does the Mexican cartel want CIA information in Africa?"

"That's what we have to find out. I'll get my team to start

looking for Charlie. They'll run face rec to see if we can catch him in an airport or in public. He might have altered his face to avoid detection. He'll have a new identity. And he wouldn't risk making contact with his old connections. But we'll find him."

Now was the time to apologize, with them sharing a common goal. It was on her to set their relationship straight. She had planned to do it on the one-hour flight. Just enough time to set the boundaries and move on to business. They needed to work as a team, not fight over stupid details like who would drive the rental as they had when they arrived in Palo Alto. Reeves conceded when she pointed out that she had defensive and evasive driving skills.

"Before we meet with your professor, I need to apologize. I'm sorry I went off last night." Her face flushed with her choice of words. "I was really angry about the whole alarm thing." She didn't think it was necessary to admit that she believed he had set the alarm because he assumed they'd be having hot sex all night. She would *not* regret that they hadn't.

"But in the end, it was a good thing. I'm here on assignment, and if there had been a real threat, I was frolicking in the pool and not doing my job."

"Your job isn't to protect me. So, I don't see what the problem is."

"The problem is that I'm on assignment to work with you. Not to sleep with you. If the Sureños are involved, this is going to get dangerous. I can't be distracted."

"Ah…so, you admit that I distract you?" He grinned.

And she hadn't realized how much his humor and smiles lessened her constant need to be on, to be in charge. He made her laugh, and for a moment, she forgot that the world was treacherous. But this wasn't the time to weaken because of a beautiful man's smile.

"You know that you do. Please don't make it harder than it has to be." She wanted to say, don't make me want you…make me regret not exploring this connection…don't grin, don't make ridiculous jokes, and don't look at me as if I am special to you.

He searched her face for clues to her feelings. He was good at reading her. She smiled, noting he had recognized her tell when she pressed her lips together.

"You're right. It is going to get dangerous. And we will both need to be on top of our game."

She reached to start the ignition. She wouldn't let him see the hurt from the kick to the gut he delivered. Their relationship always had a short shelf life. It was what she wanted, but why the raw pain and the feeling of immediate loss when he agreed? He didn't even try to convince her differently. She had hoped he would still want her, knowing it was just for the sex. She wouldn't crumble over a little romp in the pool that meant nothing. She was a CIA officer and previously a soldier who served in Afghanistan. She could handle what was thrown at her, including irresistible Reeves Hewitt.

"Was Professor Wainwright surprised to hear from you?"

"I'm not sure. He's a bit of the absentminded professor type. But he cleared his afternoon for us and seemed touched by my visit."

"I read up on him on the plane. Impressive bio. I didn't see any red flags."

He laughed a low rumble that sent waves of need through Darcy.

"Why is that funny? Anyone with his success must have an incredible drive. And universities can't be that different than any workplace with in-fighting and dirty politics."

"Wainwright lives in a mathematical theoretical realm. He's barely able to function in the real world. He's always late, never remembers little details like eating or showering. He's rather a cliché. But unlike many of the faculty, he was supportive to all of us. He was our advisor in the Theoretical Computer Science department. Academics aren't usually interested in the students or teaching. They're all about making a name for themselves and getting tenure. Students are a means to an end…assisting with the research, writing the papers to be published. But Wainwright didn't need students to move up the food chain. He was the top in his field."

"Are we wasting our time if the professor doesn't pay attention to the details of life?"

"He pays attention to mathematical theory, and Charlie's interest was always the theory of computation. Wainwright's focus. And he'll know what Charlie was working on at Berkeley and any other work. Tex and I were both more drawn to Lambda calculus and type theory."

"I've no idea what any of that means."

"We all were interested in the mathematical theory in computers."

"Thank you. So, Wainwright was closest to Charlie?"

"Strange that you ask, I've never really thought about it. But you're right. Though I doubt Charlie would have confided in the professor about his drug habit."

CHAPTER NINE

Reeves stared straight ahead but tracked Darcy's every movement as she drove to the Stanford Campus. Her curly hair was harshly pulled back in the same clip as when they first met. She wore the same navy-blue jacket and skirt. She had a fresh white blouse, the same style as yesterday. She probably owned a closet full of navy-blue suits and white blouses. He had only seen her in a suit and the heart-stopping, instant hard-on bikini, a vision that was burned into his brain for life. No woman would ever match sensual and strong Darcy Wilson in all her glory.

She probably wore jeans and a t-shirt when she hung out. He'd like to see her in tight jeans hugging her round hips and ass. Her only feminine adornment was small gold hoop earrings, probably allowed as part of the CIA dress code. Meeting all the rules and recs, she was bundled in her bureaucratic uniform. But he knew the sexy woman who hid under that uptight outfit. He wanted to undo her hair and watch the curls spring as out of control as the woman who screamed his name, lost in pleasure.

"You okay?" She glanced over at him, her voice warm with concern.

She might act like a hard-ass, but she was a big softie. And she'd take him down if she ever heard him describe her that way.

"Now that the shock is wearing off, I've got a few questions."

"Just a few?" She smirked.

"Smart-ass."

How did his sense of foreboding ease by seeing her determined face relax into a smile?

Why did women have to make it so difficult? How long would she keep denying the hot sparks between them? And what absolute bullshit that she had to focus on her job. The woman leaped out of a swimming pool, naked, to defend him against an attack. He had no doubt she could multitask. But she asked him not to make it harder for her. He wouldn't now, but he planned to make it real difficult once the case was closed. Darcy Wilson didn't like to be pushed, so he'd back off and bide his time. He might not be CIA, but he was "gifted" with a relentless focus on solving a problem. And his focus would be Darcy, and the problem would be making her happy screaming his name.

"So, what're your 'few' questions?" Her eyes briefly sought his to evaluate his mental state as the dutiful officer that she was. She wouldn't be happy to hear his thoughts.

"Why would the cartel torture Tex? Our theory that they killed him for information about *Snakes Ahead* isn't holding up. With Charlie alive, they have no reason to torture him. Are you coming to the same conclusion that he was murdered because he was looking into Charlie's death?"

"They most likely wanted to know what had he learned about Charlie's death and who he might have told."

"I'm still having trouble grasping that Charlie is alive and working with really bad guys."

"I am too. And he wasn't my friend. Once we talk with Wainwright, I'm calling for backup. Now that we know that Charlie is alive and can tie to a motive to Tex's murder, we need to proceed cautiously. We have to assume the cartel has an informant in the police department who reported that we were at Tex's and made a visit to the police department. And although I'm confident of my abilities, I'll need reinforcements to protect you from the Sureños."

"When did you plan to share your plan with me? Before or after you called the CIA?" He loved the flash of fire in her eyes.

He would never stop wanting to annoy this woman. It was some strange neuroses that would only be cured by sex with Darcy.

"I was trying to give you a little time to adjust to the shock of learning that you grieved for a friend's death that doesn't exist before I hit you with the protection detail." Her skin pinked up, and her lips compressed. "I'm sure once I make the call, the Jenkinses will be alerted. I would have already done it if we hadn't spent so much time at the police station. And I don't want us to be late for the meeting with your professor."

He was grateful that she didn't belabor the reason that the meeting with the police chief ran over was because of his shock at the chief's revelation. He had made Detective Barley repeat the information several times. Reeves had to be convinced that his friend was alive before he left. First, he had to adjust to the idea that Charlie had been murdered, and now that Charlie wasn't dead but most likely faked his death.

After the car accident, Charlie had been taken to the hospital in an ambulance. He had been pronounced dead in the ER. The body had been immediately cremated, and his ashes spread over the ocean. The ER records, including the name of the private funeral home that picked up his body for cremation, had disappeared. And with only his drug addict mother as family, no one had questioned any of the details.

"And I thought you'd be more amenable hearing it from your boss than from me."

"I'll text Nick now. They'll be rolling before we're finished with Wainwright. Did I mention that the professor loves to talk? Don't get him started on the computation theory of the mind. But, on the upside, he loves good scotch."

He reached into his jacket and texted Nick. *"Miss your ugly face, asshole. And nothing to Emily of why I'm in Palo Alto."* When had he become a Neanderthal like the Jenkins brothers?

"How would I get Wainwright started on computational theory when I know nothing about theories of computers and how they relate to the mind? And don't change the subject. I thought you'd fight me on the backup. Why the sudden change?"

"Nope. I'm not a fool. I've had enough experience with organized crime and the cartels to know that no matter how skilled you are, you have to even the odds."

She would be royally ticked if she knew he was agreeing with the extra security to protect her. She was prickly about proving herself. Now that the threat had gotten real, he wouldn't risk any harm coming to her. And the only reason he didn't fight her reasoning about being distracted in her professional role was that he never wanted to be the reason that Darcy got hurt or felt that she failed.

His phone pinged. He read Nick's text. "What the hell? The Jenkinses are already in the air and en route to Palo Alto. Your boss sent Richard the ballistics report. The gun that killed Tex had previously been used in a Sureños execution. I'm kinda surprised that Richard hasn't called me. I'm sure once he heard that the cartel was involved, he called in the troops. God, I hope it isn't both Lars and Finn with Nick. The odds of not having a fistfight when three Jenkins brothers are in the same area code are slim."

Darcy's knuckles turned white from her tight grip on the wheel. "That's bullshit. I'm the field agent on the ground, and Richard Dean hears before me…and from the director. Marwick is micromanaging this because of your relationship with Dean."

Her phone pinged, and she glanced at her phone on the console next to her Sig. "I'm probably now getting the results."

"But if they knew you were in the meeting with the police chief, they went above you to get the security in place—to give you the protection you need to do your job and keep investigating."

"It doesn't help my outrage if you're going to be reasonable. But you are owned by the 'man.'"

He was in big trouble. With all the shit going down, all he could think about was kissing her smug little smile until she melted. The idea of never kissing Darcy again was more of a loss than learning that his college friend was a criminal, possibly a terrorist. And what did that say about him?

She pulled over in an empty parking spot and reached for her phone. "I need to read this."

With her attention focused on the phone, he could appreciate all the details that made Darcy Wilson irresistible: the freckles on her nose, the mole next to her mouth that he hadn't spent any time worshiping, and the red highlights in her perfectly arched eyebrows.

"Did you know that Tex had a heart condition?"

"He was born with some sort of birth defect. He had several surgeries when he was a kid. The only reason he told Charlie and me was that his parents got him his first video game after his second surgery."

"He died of heart failure, not the gunshot wound. He had cocaine in his system. The ME thinks that his level of stimulants caused his cardiac failure. Is there any chance Tex was involved with Charlie?"

"No way. It's not totally out of the realm that Charlie got caught up in drugs. Charlie was on a full ride at Stanford. His dad split when he was a baby, leaving him with his drug addict mom. Life wasn't easy for him, surrounded by all the rich kids at Stanford. Tex had overprotective parents whom he was very close to as an only child. And Tex was a straight arrow. I never saw him drink a beer. And if he were working with Charlie, why was he investigating his death?"

She nodded as she swung back into traffic. "We're almost there. We need to discuss how to run the interview with Wainwright. The purpose is to find out anything we can about Tex or Charlie, anything about their recent work, without alerting him that I'm CIA or about the attack on the embassies."

"I told him that I was in town for a conference and was trying to catch up with old Stanford friends."

"Since he doesn't know of our stop in Santa Barbara, you'll have to act shocked if he somehow has learned of Tex's death. The agency is trying to suppress the media coverage of the murder. They don't want any publicity around the game."

"I don't plan to share the information about Charlie's resurrection either. This is strictly reconnaissance under the guise of a visit with a beloved mentor. Wainwright knew the three of us.

And his perspective and memories will be different than mine. He also is the only other person who understood how we developed the game. Not that he was privy to the actual code."

"Let's introduce me as a colleague from Seattle. We are both attending the same conference."

"Sure, and when Wainwright asks you about the conference?" Reeves knew that a smart cookie CIA officer already knew what the best cover was. He enjoyed waiting her out.

"Good point. I'll have to be your girlfriend who came to the conference for a break." Her lips were pressed together.

"You think that's the best cover? I'm not sure Wainwright would believe we're together. You're going to have to act nice and friendly."

"Don't be an ass. And don't get carried away with the affection. Remember I'm carrying."

She now had the Sig that the guard had brought to the front door last night when she and Reeves were in the pool.

"No, honeybunch. I would never put you in an uncomfortable situation with unwanted love and affection. I know how miserable it would make you."

She was white-knuckling the steering wheel again. She must care, or she wouldn't react. Sure, and giraffes flew.

CHAPTER TEN

Reeves gently placed his hand on Darcy's back to escort her into Professor Wainwright's office. She gritted her teeth, knowing how much Reeves would enjoy this charade. The room was large with a bank of wide windows that provided an impressive view of the campus. A computer was placed center on a small desk that faced the window. Shelves, heavy with books, lined two walls; a work table was in the middle of the room. Books, stacks of papers, old coffee cups, and foam containers were scattered on both the wood table and the scarred desk, giving the room a musty stench. Several pairs of reading glasses lay in the middle of the chaos.

Wainwright pushed away from his desk and moved toward them, his hands open in welcome. For all the empty food containers, the professor was a lean, wiry man in his mid-sixties. His glasses were shoved on the top of his disheveled, salt-and-pepper hair; his rumpled Oxford shirt was partially tucked into his dress pants. His receding hairline emphasized his prominent forehead and beak nose. He barely resembled his distinguished faculty picture on the Stanford website, more like a harried appliance salesman.

"Reeves, you haven't changed a bit."

Darcy felt the rumble of Reeve's laughter shooting sparks of awareness down her spine.

"My hair's a bit shorter." Reeves shook hands with Wainwright, who eyed Darcy while grinning at Reeves. "Darcy, meet Professor

Wainwright. He deserves credit for putting up with Tex, Charlie, and me when no other faculty would."

"A great exaggeration. I was lucky to have the three brightest stars, all interested in computational theory."

Something didn't ring true about his false modesty. He was at the top of the food chain at a prestigious university.

"Professor Wainwright, this is the love of my life—my girlfriend, Darcy Wilson." Reeves smiled down at her, his eyes shining with pride as if he meant his words.

She was going to pound him for making her insides get all mushy just from his warm gaze. She offered her hand to the professor. Handshakes were a good way to gauge the emotional state of an adversary.

His thin hands were clammy, and he barely grasped her hand. Either he was anxious around women or socially awkward. There was no reason for him to be nervous. She noted no wedding ring and no family pictures anywhere in his office.

"Come sit down." He pointed to the table in the center of the room. "I want to hear what you've been working on, Reeves. I always thought you would stay in academics. You were the best of the group at translating complex theory to the undergrad students."

"Honey, why don't you sit here?" Reeves held the chair that gave her a view of the door and the room, directly across from Wainwright. A point for Reeves for situational awareness.

"As you must know, Darcy, Reeves had a following of the female students. He's quite the charmer with the women."

Reeves's cheeks flushed. Interesting. She didn't know anything about his dating life. He wasn't involved now because he wasn't the sort of man to cheat. And she realized at the moment how much she trusted him.

"I'm sorry, Darcy. I shouldn't bring up Reeves's past." His smile didn't meet his eyes. Was he testing their relationship, or was he as awkward as Reeves described? "I'm awful at chit-chat. I'm much better at discussing my work than..."

She squeezed Reeves's hand, which rested on the table. "I'm grateful that Reeves was unattached when I met him."

She waited to see the glint of amusement in Reeves's dark eyes. His eyes were shuttered. And she was surprised by her feeling of loss. She had gotten used to his openness. When he shut her out, it hurt.

He took her hand and placed it on his muscular thigh, then covered it with his.

"Today calls for a celebration. Not often I have one of my best students come to visit. I want to hear all the news about you and Tex." Wainwright walked to the tall file cabinet, pulled out a drawer, and held up a bottle of Macallan scotch. He shoved aside a stack of papers on the top of the cabinet to find a place for the bottle before producing three glasses.

"Thank you, Professor Wainwright, but I must decline. I'm allergic to malt liquor." Darcy wasn't allergic to scotch and would have enjoyed the expensive blend. But she never drank on the job.

"What a shame. I've never heard of such an allergy."

"It's true. Darcy with hives is not a pretty sight. Isn't that right, honey?"

She squeezed his thigh hard. Reeves stared at her hand before his lips lifted in a small smile.

Wainwright handed Reeves a very generous pour before he sat across from Darcy. His drink was less than half of Reeves's.

"Reeves described how wonderful you were to him and his friends. Must have been a challenge dealing with these super-smart, arrogant men." She paused to look closely at his face for a reaction. "What a tragedy with Charlie's accident to lose one of your brilliant students. It must have been such a shock and a loss for you. Wasn't he your top student in computational theory? I know Reeves and Tex were more into Lambda."

"I always thought Charlie would be my protégé."

"I'm surprised then that you didn't stay in touch?" Reeves pitched his voice enough not to make it sound like a direct question.

Darcy repressed any smile from appearing. She and Reeves were a good team.

"We did for a while, but then he dropped off the radar. Just disappeared. I assume that was when he started using drugs."

"Reeves never believed that Charlie would use drugs. Isn't that so, honey? You thought the press just wanted a sensational story. A millionaire cocaine addict to pander to the theme of the excesses of the young and wealthy techies in Silicon Valley."

"I can't believe Charlie would use…especially cocaine. Our brains are already spinning faster than everyone else. You believed the story? Or did you hear something else?"

"Why all these questions now about Charlie? He's been gone almost ten years."

"I'm sorry, Professor Wainwright. It's my fault, but I know how much Reeves has grieved Charlie's death. I guess I was hoping he could find closure by coming back here."

"Of course. Let's talk about happier things. When are you getting married? And do you plan to have a family?"

Either the man was very skilled or completely socially inept. Who asked about children after just meeting a woman?

"Darcy wants an enormous wedding. She has a large extended family, so it's going to be big and expensive." How did he know about her family and what kind of wedding she always imagined?

"Now, Reeves, don't start on the budget again. For all his money, he can be a miser. Do you have children? Is that why you're interested in families?"

"No, I never married. Seemed I was destined to guide the next generation of mathematicians."

Darcy couldn't get a clear read on this man who Reeves esteemed. Reeves was very intuitive for a man. But he had been an immature and impressionable student when he formed his opinion of his mentor.

"Darcy and I want a large family. She wants to have a brood of little Reeveses, right, babe? She is tired of selling cosmetics at Nordstrom. It's where I met her. I was shopping for my mom and sisters."

Darcy didn't know whether to laugh or throat punch him. She shouldn't be entertained by his ability to lie with such facility. He'd be great in the CIA. And he loved teasing her, knowing exactly how to poke fun at her. He had only known her little more than twenty-four hours, but he was already more adept than her brothers at getting under her skin. And adept at unfreezing her libido, which had been in deep storage until meeting him.

"You must still be in touch with Tex since you have to communicate about your shared ownership of the game." The professor looked over his glass at Reeves.

"Now that it's managed by Rocket Games, Tex and I don't have any reason to be in touch. And I haven't heard anything from him in years. How about you? Any contact?"

"Nothing. I don't even know who he's working for or what he's working on."

Darcy pasted an interested look on her face as the men discussed their different colleague's work. At least Reeves hadn't given her a role that demanded that she had to pretend to understand any of the mathematical theories the men debated.

Watching Reeves sit forward, his face lit with enthusiasm by talking about programming and something about Turing complete, she understood his bond with Wainwright.

After fifteen minutes of the men's shop talk, Darcy nudged Reeves with her knee. She was antsy to check in with her CIA support team and Nick Jenkins.

She felt unsure about the professor. He knew more about Charlie than he was willing to share. He was quite adept at changing the subject. But he gave them nothing to help with the investigation.

After fake promises to not let as much time lapse before the next meeting, she and Reeves went outside where she could take a deep breath. The air in the office had been stifling, or maybe it was the mathematics snooze fest, or maybe it was the fact that she kept waiting for cockroaches to crawl out of one of the containers.

Reeves leaned on her as they walked side by side down the sidewalk.

"Knock it off. No need to keep playing the devoted boyfriend. You're lucky I don't kick your butt for saying that BS about wanting little Reeveses."

Reeves weaved against her, almost knocking her off her feet.

She grabbed his arm to support him. His face was pale, and his pupils dilated.

"The scotch just hit me." His words were garbled.

His eyes rolled backward before he passed out and fell against her. She struggled but couldn't hold him upright. She lowered him onto the sidewalk and removed his shoulder bag for comfort, and then his entire body twitched in uncoordinated spasms. His eyes were open but unaware. Frothy white foam formed around his mouth. My God, he was having a seizure.

"Help me. Call 911!" Darcy shouted out to a young woman with a backpack texting. The student stopped walking and immediately dialed her phone.

Darcy checked his pulse. It was racing. She didn't know if Reeves had a seizure disorder or he had been poisoned. Either way, he needed immediate medical attention. Now. She knelt next to him and lifted his head onto her lap to prevent him from injuring himself on the cement. She knew enough not to put anything in his mouth or try to restrain him, but that was it for the emergency care. "Stay with me, Reeves. I'm going to get you to the hospital."

Darcy sorted through the possible ways Reeves could have ingested poison. He hadn't been in contact with anyone except the chief of police and the professor to have absorbed the poison through his skin. And they both ate the same breakfast on the flight. It had to be in the scotch. That was the only difference in their experiences and intake.

"The ambulance is less than five minutes away." The student stood over them. "What can I do to help?"

Reeves's muscles suddenly tightened, throwing his head hard against her lap. His breathing changed to rapid and shallow, his eyes vacant. Terror filled her lungs, making it hard to take in air as she helplessly watched him suffer through another seizure. There was nothing she could do to stop the seizures. She hated feeling that way. She texted Nick Jenkins to ask about Reeves's medical conditions. With their deep investigation into him, she never saw any medical problems.

Her entire being tightened, adrenaline shooting through her

with a need to act. He would not die on her watch. Time slowed as she waited in agony for the seizure to stop, knowing not to interfere unless he stopped breathing.

"University Hospital is less than a mile away. They'll be here soon." The concerned student, like Darcy, was powerless to intervene.

She silently prayed when she heard the sirens. *Please, God, let him live.* She couldn't lose him when she just discovered how wonderful he was.

Two medics rushed toward her, pushing a gurney. The taller one asked questions as they lifted an unconscious Reeves onto the stretcher. Darcy's ignorance of Reeves's medical history was abominable. She passed Jenkins's contact info. They'd be able to sort it out.

Darcy's knees buckled when she stood. Now that the seizure had stopped, he lay still on the gurney, which was as frightening as the spasms. The energetic man lifeless was more terrifying than any firefight in Afghanistan. His calm state might be a good sign that the seizures had stopped. But if he had been poisoned, he could be going into heart failure as Tex had.

Both medics worked in harmony in the small space. The shorter attendant put an oxygen mask on Reeves as the taller man hooked him up to monitors and attached a blood pressure cuff.

"Is he going into heart failure?"

The taller one jerked his head up from shining a light into Reeves's pupils. "He's stable."

"Where are you taking him? I want to follow you to the hospital."

"To University Hospital."

She flashed her badge. "There is a chance that he has been poisoned. You need to run blood tests immediately. And keep your guard up."

And with a nod from the man who seemed to be in charge, he closed the doors.

Darcy's heart constricted in fear and pain from the separation from Reeves.

She ran the fifty yards to the SUV. Jumping into the vehicle, she threw the car into reverse. Never losing sight of the ambulance, she sped down the campus street. She reached for her phone in her purse and hit speed dial for her team.

"Hewitt is down. He had a seizure after our meeting with Wainwright. Not sure if it is poison or if he has a seizure disorder. I'm headed to the hospital. Notify the director and Nick Jenkins. Tell Jenkins to meet me at the Stanford Hospital and to get someone to Wainwright's office. I'm following the ambulance now."

Had Wainwright poisoned Reeves? She had watched the professor pour the scotch from the container into the glasses. He didn't have an opportunity to poison Reeves's drink. The only conclusion was that both men had been poisoned. She had no clear motive for an attack on the professor except from his link to Reeves and the other men.

She sped up as she raced through the intersection to avoid being stuck at a red light. She didn't see the SUV coming at her until it was too late. He slammed into her, hitting her with such velocity that her car spun in the opposite direction as her head ricocheted off the airbag and then slammed into the headrest from the impact.

She fought the blackness sneaking into her periphery. Her last thought was that she had failed to protect Reeves.

CHAPTER ELEVEN

Darcy squinted, trying to get her brain to fire. There was a connectivity lapse like slow Wi-Fi. White drapes, antiseptic smell, beeping sounds, the shuffle of feet, and shouts of voices. She was still in the emergency room.

A memory flashed of a fist meeting her face before she woke up in an ambulance. He'd used his car to jerk her neck like a rubber band, then she'd slammed her head into the airbag and then into the headrest. As if that wasn't enough, the asswipe had knocked her out after t-boning her. Staggering out of the SUV, she'd been unable to react fast enough to defend herself before she hit the cement.

"You're awake?" A deep bass voice startled her. She lurched toward the sound, causing blinding agony. She was definitely off her game if she hadn't noticed the enormous man sitting next to her bed. Her head hurt like a son of a gun.

"I'm Nick Jenkins."

"Reeves?" Her voice cracked with the emotion clogging her throat. All the terror of the minutes watching Reeves have seizures came back in awful precision. "Is he…"

She didn't want to imagine the world without Reeves. Her world without him. He couldn't be dead. She would feel it, wouldn't she?

"Kidnapped."

Darcy shot upright, ignoring the twirling room, the atomic pain in her head, and the acute throbbing in her arm. She gazed down at the splint keeping her left arm pinned against her chest. Memories of the ER flashed through her mind. Thank God it was her left shoulder that had been dislocated, not affecting her shooting arm.

"Get me out of here. Now!" she shouted and immediately regretted her rash behavior since the loud decibels pierced like a laser knife to her brain.

"Reeves was poisoned?" She knew the answer and already was rebuking herself. She had allowed her feelings for him to block her judgment. She should have spotted the entire setup as it was going down.

"We're assuming he was poisoned with cocaine—the same found in Thompson's body. Which would account for the seizures."

She was slow on the uptake from the pain and whatever they gave her to fix her shoulder. She needed caffeine, then she'd be firing on all cylinders. The ambulance wasn't real, but his seizures were.

She covered her mouth and breathed through her nose to fight the nausea creeping up her throat.

"I let them abduct him. I considered riding with him in the ambulance, but the space was small, and I didn't want to inhibit their ability to take care of him. I never for one second questioned their legitimacy. A random student called 911. Nothing raised any flags."

If anything happened to Reeves, she would never recover. "They were completely professional. They gave him oxygen and hooked him up to monitors." The terrible event replayed in her mind.

"They were real EMTs. We found them gagged and tied up with the ambulance in the Hewlett Packard garage."

She shoved the blanket down, causing excruciating agony to detonate in her arm. She tugged at the hospital gown that was hitched up to her thighs. She had allowed Reeves to be kidnapped when he couldn't defend himself.

"Did you pick up Wainwright? The poison has to have been in the scotch. I didn't have any, but Reeves had a huge amount. Wainwright filled his glass, the bastard."

"Wainwright also got sick. His assistant found him vomiting and shaky."

"Someone got into Wainwright's office and poisoned the scotch?" She rubbed her temples, trying to stop the aching pain that was reverberating like a jackhammer to focus on the problem.

"Only your team and mine knew about our meeting with Wainwright. We have to stop the local police from touching the evidence. This is a federal case now. I have jurisdiction, and we need to get that scotch out of police custody."

"Hey, hold up. You aren't discharged yet."

"Then get me discharged." She had to find Reeves before they tortured him and then shot him point-blank.

"You have a concussion and a dislocated shoulder and possibly a broken nose. Your boss, the director, has already made it clear that this is a CIA operation with Jenkins Security."

"Get this fucking rail down." Her hands shook as she tried to release the stupid-ass railing. She had cleaned up her swearing when she joined the CIA, but today she didn't give a flying fuck. Being raised with a pack of wolves and then in the Army had taught her very colorful and clear ways to communicate.

He pushed it easily, lowering the rail. "It might be better if you rested."

"And would you rest if Emily was missing?" She stopped before she started to roll her eyes, knowing it would hurt like a mother.

"How do you know about Emily?" He glowered over her, all big and burly, his dark eyes piercing hers. And she wasn't in the least impressed.

"CIA. I know everything about Jenkins Security." She didn't admit that she had listened to Reeves's and his conversation. She also had delved into Jenkins Security to see if they were a front to launder money from Reeves's side gigs. Security companies run by ex-military were plentiful and didn't always care about their clients' real business as long as they got a paycheck and a fix of adrenaline.

She swung her legs, which seemed to be the only part of her body that wasn't screaming at her. "I didn't stop them. I let them slam the door and abduct him."

"You did what any of us would have done. You were attempting to save his life."

"You can quit the bullshit. We all know his kidnapping is on me. I should have called for backup, put him in a safe house when we found Tex."

"It isn't bullshit. I didn't think it was necessary, and neither did Reeves. He wouldn't want you second-guessing your decision. I reassured his sister that he was safe. So don't put all the blame on your little old self. There's plenty to go around."

"We can have a pity party later."

He laughed. "No touchy-feely, huh?"

"Nope. Army and four brothers knock it right out of you."

"We have something in common with all the brothers. But not the Army, dogface." His lips lifted in the smallest of a smile. "Not that the name applies to you."

One of the many insulting names different branches gave to each other. Dogface was an insult leveled at Army members.

"The way my face feels, I bet it does apply. I'm not planning on looking in a mirror for a while. Can you find my clothes? They should be in a bag somewhere."

"They're covered in blood from the guy decking you. I bought you a t-shirt and flip-flops at the gift store, but you'll have to wear your skirt."

"As long as I don't have to get into the heels, it's all good." She let her legs dangle, waiting for the room to stop spinning like a damn tilt-a-whirl.

"And I'm assuming there are no leads from the ambulance because the cameras just happened to be off in the very big and very busy garage. And Reeves's phone?"

"Nothing. It is trashed or they took out the SIM card. The same for yours. We tried to get a location on your phone and Reeves's computer, but nothing."

"They didn't hit me to stop me from following the ambulance." She placed one foot on the floor and waited before putting her whole weight down. She leaned heavily against the bed, letting the waves of nausea wash over her and the spasms in her temple slow down.

"I'm assuming they wanted Reeves's computer. They took your phone and your Sig too."

"I took his bag off his shoulder when he was seizing." Tears welled behind her eyes. Damn, she would not look weak in front of Nick Jenkins.

She couldn't allow herself to consider how easily they could have overdosed Reeves. And he might be dead.

"They could have overdosed Reeves as they did Tex."

"I bet they didn't know that Tex had a heart condition," Nick said. "Reeves is healthy. He's alive."

She nodded and regretted it when the room spun from the slight motion.

"If they wanted Reeves dead, they would have killed him."

Darcy was glad that Nick Jenkins didn't sugarcoat it for her, accepting that she could handle whatever came at her.

"And they can't access Reeves's computer without Reeves, so they have to keep him alive." Hope blossomed in her aching body. "We need to find him now. Before he becomes expendable. Let's go."

"I can keep you updated without you leaving the hospital."

And she thought it had registered with Jenkins that she was no fragile flower. She started to raise her hand and then stopped midair at the pain and the constriction of the splint. "I'm going to leave, with or without your assistance."

"Does Reeves know what a PITA you are?"

"Of course not. He thinks I'm charming."

He snorted, shaking his head. "You're a lot like my sisters."

In the midst of all of her misery, his comment made her feel better.

He handed her the t-shirt and dropped the flip-flops in front of her feet. "I'll get the nurse to help you get dressed. And then I'll get you discharged."

She sat on the edge of the bed now that the show was over for Jenkins. Her pain was nothing in comparison to what Reeves was enduring. Tex's bruised face flashed before her eyes. She would find Reeves or die trying.

CHAPTER TWELVE

Reeves was trapped in a nightmare. He couldn't escape. He spiraled down into the deep, dark tunnel. The walls and ceilings had collapsed, burying him in a black hell. He couldn't suck air into his lungs. He fought the sensation of being suffocated. Death tightened the vise on his chest. Struggling to wake up and end the torture, he pushed against the mud to no avail. His arms and legs were heavy and immobile. He had to escape, had to reach the woman to save her.

Men's loud voices in the distance stirred him out of the unending hallucination. It would be easy to surrender and drift away. His eyes fluttered shut, sinking back into the misery until an angry voice startled him.

"He'll kill you if this bastard dies like the last one. You shouldn't have put the whole fucking amount in the scotch."

"Who knew a tech nerd would drink so much."

The mention of tech nerd and scotch roused Reeves into total alertness. He lay still, his eyes closed as he strained to follow every word. Trying hard to track their words that came in and out like static in a bad speaker. Their voices grew closer. He heard the shuffle of their feet and heavy breathing. They were standing over him, staring at him?

"The boss must be desperate to have come up with such a stupid-ass idea of using C to give the dude seizures."

"It's good the nerd ain't dead, cuz then you would be too, bro."

Reeves fought every urge to move, to hide any hint of being awake. Reeves knew his brain was fried from the cocaine because he couldn't remember having seizures and how that helped the fuckers capture him. However, they got him here, wherever here was, and he was a prisoner.

"What the fuck? Who goes into business with a white dude who wants to be called '*mandamás*,' as if he's the top dog of the Sureños? The freak had some serious shit and a death wish going on."

That greasy French fry smell when driving by a fast-food drive-through wafted over Reeves. His captors weren't into healthy eating. No surprise there.

"What dumb fucker offs himself mixing snow with Xanax? The dude was supposed to be such a genius. Now, we've only got this guy. The Sureños and the boss needed him to do the computer shit. And if he fails…we're all in deep to…those Russian fuckers."

"You better wake him up and give him some water. I'll text Galina. She is one cold bitch."

"Can't believe you had to sucker punch that CIA bitch to get his computer."

"I could feel the cartilage break when I connected with her skank face. She's got balls to get out of the car after I T-boned her. Man, I accelerated before I slammed into her."

Reeves was wide awake. Adrenaline mainlining through his blood did that. *Darcy.* They had T-boned her, then the bastard had hit her. The asshole was so dead for bragging that he broke her nose. Reeves was primed to choke the life out of the bastard. The only good news was that he knew that Darcy was alive, and they hadn't decided to give her seizures with that cocaine mixture. Small blessings in this shithole situation.

Reeves strained to remember how he and Darcy had become separated. His last memory was falling against Darcy, thinking he was becoming a lightweight who couldn't hold a single tumbler of scotch. Flashes of Darcy cradling his head in her lap and feeling as if he were floating were all that he had. Nothing else.

He tried to sort out the dudes' information, but his razor-sharp focus was dulled like a butter knife. He already knew that the Sureños were involved, but these dimwits worked for a "boss" aligned with the gang and somehow with the Russians.

Was "the white dude" Charlie who offed himself? But they'd learned that Charlie was alive, which meant that it had to be Tex. But that didn't add up since someone killed Tex, and they said this white dude offed himself mixing cocaine with Xanax. Reeves's head hurt from his attempt to concentrate and sort through the information.

It didn't matter who was behind his capture. Darcy and the Jenkinses would figure it out. Reeves had to get access to his computer and send Darcy a message with his GPS. And then he had to escape. Not that much to handle when he probably couldn't stand or remember his password.

"Hey, asshole, wake up." Reeves's arm was yanked almost out of his shoulder. He could feel McDonald's breath on his face.

"Dump the water on him."

Shit. Time to give up the possum game. Reeves slowly opened one eye, preparing for the worst.

"Get up and drink the water. You need to get to work if you want to see your CIA girlfriend again."

Reeves opened both eyes, trying to avoid getting any closer than absolutely necessary to sit up. An obese guy with caramel-colored skin and a do-rag on his head, keeping his dreadlocks in place, hovered over Reeves.

"You going to release me after I show you the difference in Python versus Java code?" He believed that they planned for him to see Darcy as much as he believed they were the tech team.

McDonald shot a blank look at his partner, who was the muscle. He wore a tight green t-shirt advertising a local gym, his blond hair in a military cut, full sleeves of colorful tats on both arms. Reeves didn't recognize the tattoos—were they Sureños gang tats?

"Sure. Once you hold down the water, we've got grub for you." The muscle nodded toward the table holding bags of drive-through food.

He would never be able to eat fast food again. "Thanks."

Reeves waited for the room to not tilt and the acid crawling up his throat to stop. He swung around to sit on the edge of the steel cot. Holding his hands to his head, he groaned, overdramatizing how badly he felt. He wanted his captors to underestimate him and his training. Unfortunately, he didn't need to act much. Coming down from the drug cocktail was playing havoc with his nervous system. Every sound, smell, and touch was magnified to the point of pain.

Keeping his head down, he scanned the room from underneath his hands.

He was in an eight-by-ten room with no windows, nothing but his cot, a metal table, chairs, and the bags of food and water bottles. Oh, and his computer bag. The door lock from this angle looked to be a Schlage Encode. Easy-peasy. And there was no urinal. All adding up in his favor.

"Galina should be here soon." McDonald took Reeves's arm and jerked him up. "Time to show off all that genius."

"I don't need to show off to anyone." Reeves didn't like the guy's sweaty fingers squeezing his arm.

McDonald pulled out a Glock from the back of his jeans. "Get over to the table by your bag. Not sure what the big deal is about one computer. We had to go to a lot of trouble to get it."

The reminder of what they had done to Darcy to get his computer fueled his anger to take these assholes down. They were playing in his world and didn't stand a chance. And they had made a fatal mistake by allowing him his computer.

"I need to take a piss after you made me drink all the water." He needed to do a little reconnaissance if he planned to get the hell out of here.

The two shared a look before McDonald wrenched his arm again. The violent motion set off the shooting pain behind his eyes and the nausea. Reeves took a slow breath, managing not to fight back and break the guy's arm. He had never actually broken anyone's limbs, but he had practiced the technique. And it would give him great pleasure to watch this guy drop and cry like a baby.

Reeves was ready to pull his arm out of the guy's hand when he remembered he was supposed to be a nerd who was still feeling the effects of the cocaine.

Reeves swayed against Muscle, ramming his whole weight into the guy. "Sorry, I'm still a bit woozy from whatever you gave me to get my cooperation."

"Smart-ass. You got the amount you needed."

Now, Reeves had to hurt McDonald for the drugs and Muscle for touching Darcy. Just as soon as the room stopped spinning and he didn't want to hurl, he'd have a plan.

CHAPTER THIRTEEN

Darcy awoke when the car stopped at the gate to a two-story, ranch-style house on the shores of a shimmering lake. The bright sun's reflection hurt like a needle stab to her eyes. Her headache had gone from excruciating to a dull throb. She could handle the headache once she had coffee. Caffeine fixed most problems.

She crashed immediately in the front seat after walking from the ER to the car. She had refused a wheelchair beyond the curb, not wanting to be perceived as weak by the Jenkins, but then slept, oblivious to the car ride. Talk about situational awareness. And then it dawned on her—she fully trusted Nick Jenkins to cover her.

"Are we still in Palo Alto?"

If they were at a distance from town, how could they quickly pivot when they got the information on Reeves? The well-tended waterfront houses looked more like an upper-class suburb than a college campus.

"We're between Palo Alto and Mountain View, less than five miles from the campus. This is the house Jordan, Dean's oldest daughter, lived in when she was a student at Stanford. Jenkins Security installed all the latest in security when she resided here. Richard, also a Stanford graduate, is on the board of trustees and attends regular meetings, and periodically gives special seminars for the faculty and graduate students. Since he frequently stays here, the house has the most current surveillance equipment and the capacity to function as a safe house. It will be our temporary headquarters."

An armed man opened the gate.

"By the look of the guard's Glock 17, you aren't solely relying on tech." She approved but didn't say anything. Nick Jenkins didn't need approval. The man knew his business.

"Hell, no. We're all trained for combat, not cybercrime. That's Reeves's job."

"But without Reeves…" She hated that her voice quivered just mentioning his name. "We need top tech on this. Molly is the best at the CIA, but she is tasked with the malware search at the moment. I'll call the director and see if he'd be willing to reassign Molly to our team." She'd use her connection to Richard Dean to get what she needed for Reeves.

"No need for Molly. Izzy Benson is already on board. She's my brother Sten's fiancée, a female version of Reeves. Izzy is NSA's superstar, so we're covered. Reeves is family. Everyone is working to bring him home."

Nick's words eased the persistent panic in every breath she took since she'd learned of Reeves's abduction. She wasn't alone. Reeves wasn't alone. He had a family with incredible skills and resources.

She slowed her breathing, trying to suppress the image of Tex's battered body that replayed in her brain. Knowing the Sureños could be torturing Reeves accomplished nothing. She usually could compartmentalize, but her feelings for the sensitive and caring man were messing with her head. She was a trained CIA officer. *Get a grip, Darcy.*

"It is most likely that the Sureños are holding Reeves. And they're being directed by an unknown partner. If we're lucky, their partner hasn't sent more manpower to assist the Sureños."

Nick pulled the SUV in front of the home's entrance. He killed the engine and turned. "We're already watching all possible entries into the city. This has cartel written all over it with the drugging, kidnapping, assassination, but the big question that remains is who is paying for the services of the Sureños?"

"The Sureños wouldn't commit blatant acts of terrorism. They might sell guns to our enemies, but attacking the embassies is bad for business and calls attention to their activities. My money is on Russia, who is very interested in the natural resources that Africa has to offer. They're doing exactly what they did in the Ukraine—offering assistance before they slowly overtake the infrastructure, and their military is insinuated to take control. And how better to solidify their position than by knowing their enemies' covert intelligence?"

"Our team's focus is to get Reeves out of the hands of the scumbags. The whole link between the Sureños and Russia is more within the CIA's purview. But I'm expecting you have some experience taking out the garbage?"

Now, this was a mission she could wrap her head around. She almost smiled, but it hurt too much to move her face. "Yeah, I've had my share of scumbags. And I need a Sig, but I can work with a Glock 17."

"Like the attitude." He jumped out of the car, ducking his head inside to talk with her. "I'll give you a hand down. You'll find your equilibrium is off if you've never been in a sling. You'll learn pretty quick that two arms are a big help to balance."

Darcy nodded. She had to swallow her pride. Never easy for her, and then to be forced to accept help. Also, not her greatest strength.

Nick opened her door and held out his hand. She swung her legs around and took his hand.

"It sucks to be injured. I've been there."

"Thanks."

She followed him into the house, thinking of when she had followed Reeves into another safe house. Her body had stored the memories of their time in the pool, her skin on fire by his sensual and tender touch, the wiry hair on his chest abrading her nipples, his mouth on her. She would find Reeves. He wouldn't escape her. He owed her a night together.

"We've set you up in one of the bedrooms. It's this way." Nick gestured to the clear circular steps. "I'll wake you when we have intelligible action."

Like Merissa Storm's, the main floor had wall-to-wall

windows to view the lake and a surrounding outside deck to take advantage of California's sunny clime. It was an open-floor plan with three steps up to the main floor and then a stairwell to the bedrooms.

"Thanks, but I'm ready to work. Can I get a cup of coffee?" Darcy headed toward the kitchen, where she spotted a coffee maker. A long marble-top island divided the kitchen from the living room.

Two dark-haired Nick look-alikes came into the living room from a room on the main floor. The genes were potent in the Jenkins family. They were all broad, big men with sharp features, piercing eyes, and determined chins that spoke of will and stubbornness. They had the arrogance that only spec forces emitted. Total confidence in who they were and their impressive capabilities. In the presence of such powerful men, relief washed over Darcy. These men would succeed in hunting Reeves's captors. Failure wasn't in their DNA.

"Hey, looks as if you took one for the team." He offered his large hand. "I'm Finn Jenkins, and this is my baby brother, Lars."

Darcy had to look up to see baby Lars. She shook their hands, both callused and firm.

"We've all been waiting to meet the woman who was willing to put Reeves on the terrorist watch list." Lars's eyes sparkled in amusement.

It did sound rather lame now that she knew Reeves. But she wasn't backing down. Used to her brothers' challenging humor, she recognized Lars's ploy.

"I never added him to the list. But it's never too late to add names." She raised her eyebrow and immediately regretted the motion. She tried to hide the grimace, but there was no fooling these men.

"Let me get you some ibuprofen. Dislocated shoulders hurt like a son of…"

Darcy thought it was rather sweet that Finn stopped cursing for her sake. He would learn pretty quickly that nothing he said could shock her.

"It could be worse. It could be your gun hand." Lars walked behind the island. "You want coffee, right? How do you take it?"

"Black, please."

She didn't miss that the men didn't mention Reeves. "No leads?"

Nick put his hands into his worn jeans. "Nada yet. This is the worst part. The waiting."

Finn returned with a bottle of pills and then, realizing that she couldn't easily open the bottle with her left arm pinned against her chest, took out two and handed them to her. She dry swallowed them.

It was worth it to see the surprise on all three of the brothers' faces. They hadn't seen anything yet.

"Reeves maybe with a spook…but a dogface, a tough-ass spook? Didn't see that coming." Finn had the same glint in his bright eyes as Lars.

Darcy didn't have the energy to correct Finn that she and Reeves weren't a couple.

"Does Reeves have some sort of SERE—Survival, Evasion, Resistance, and Escape training to withstand the torture?" It would be a lot easier, and a lot less painful, for Darcy to remain in denial of what the Sureños were capable of. Her job was to assess the risk to Reeves and his survival.

Nick and Finn's shared look was enough of an answer. "We never considered it for Reeves since he's tech, not an operator."

"Hey, I get it." She tried to raise her hands and stopped herself. "I'm not judging."

Lars came around the island and handed her a steaming cup of java. She inhaled the dark scent before taking her first sip. "Thank you."

"Caffeine is as necessary as C4 for a successful mission." Finn winked at her.

"Finn was a SEAL, and they're really into blowing things up," Lars deadpanned.

"We take our demolition skills seriously." The macho joking was familiar and comforting since it reminded her of home and her brothers.

"Reeves has a license to carry, but I'm assuming he's never fired his pistol in a live situation."

"He's improved at the shooting range, but his ability to kill someone?" Finn shrugged his shoulders. "He's not trained to react, but he's a quick study. He'll handle himself if he has to."

"I agree with Finn's assessment. Reeves is analytical. He'll do an assessment, weigh his options and, if his best option for survival is to stop the bad guys, he won't hesitate," Nick said.

"I hope that it doesn't come down to Reeves having to be in a firefight. Reeves doesn't need that on his conscience." She was attracted to more about Reeves than the obvious fact that he was sexy as hell—he wasn't like the men she knew. But she hadn't realized until now that part of her need for him was because he wasn't hardened. He didn't have blood on his hands as she and other soldiers did. And she never wanted him to. She liked him as he was, a nerdy geek and a tender, hot man.

CHAPTER FOURTEEN

Reeves waited behind McDonald for him to unlock the door that kept him prisoner. Confident that Reeves could never make it to the door or have the opportunity to use the seven-digit code, or just plain stupid, McDonald made no effort to safeguard the code.

"Whoa, sorry. I'm so damn dizzy."

Reeves fell against McDonald, interrupting the keypad sequence, forcing McDonald to repeat the code to reinforce the numbers in his drug-addled brain and simply to piss the guy off. Maintaining your captors off-balance was one strategy, and the other was to pit them against each other. If he hadn't been poisoned, he'd already have developed a plan. He wanted out now. He wanted Darcy. And he wanted to see these assholes behind bars for the rest of their sorry lives.

McDonald held the door for Reeves to leave his cell/room. Reeves walked into the rectangular cement room with hanging fluorescent lights. He had no memory of being carried through the empty warehouse. Probably wouldn't be empty for long. Since the Sureños dealt in arms and drugs, this spot likely served as a secure holding area to store their goods. The Sureños weren't very creative in where they stashed their captives. Warehouses were almost redundant in the business of kidnapping.

Reeves followed McDonald to the bathroom, which was on the opposite side of the room. McDonald's heavy shuffle echoed off the thirty-foot ceiling.

McDonald pushed the door open and shoved Reeves into a small, dingy bathroom. It smelled like a gas station toilet. The linoleum floor was cracked, the previously white sink was gray with rust marks around the handles, and the toilet seat and rim were covered in things Reeves didn't want to consider. A purple sanitizer was attached to the filthy toilet in an attempt to obliterate the awful smell. The harsh chemical sanitizer, scented to mimic grapes, made Reeves gag and his eyes water.

"Take a piss," McDonald barked.

"You're going to watch me?"

McDonald's face didn't change.

"FYI, I'm cool with your choice. But I'm not into dudes." Always worked with these macho types to insult their manhood.

"Shut the fuck up. Or I'll shut you up."

"Tsk, tsk. Didn't your mother teach you any manners?"

McDonald pulled his Glock from his jeans. "Take a piss, now!"

Reeves turned and unzipped his fly. What the hell was he thinking by provoking the asshole? Focus. This wasn't the time. Yet. He stored the idea for future reference of taking one out in the bathroom.

"You could just have said 'please.'"

At the sight of the gangbanger's Glock, Reeves suddenly remembered that his Glock was in his computer bag. He had no idea if the guys confiscated the firearm since he had no memory of anything after the scotch. Talk about having a cocaine hangover; he'd lost track of everything, including his firearm. In his defense, this was the first time he had needed to carry a gun. His world was protected, and his only threats were cyber. The Jenkinses would be disappointed to know that despite all of their training, he lost track of his piece. But he'd been poisoned and had seizures, so he hoped it gave him a pass. He really needed a coffee to jumpstart his brain.

Nick had made sure that Reeves had the latest weapon—a Glock 19 Gen 5, faster and with more firepower than McDonald's older Glock 17. And one rule of thumb with gangbangers was they knew their firearms. His Glock 19 would give him a psychological advantage, but he was still at a disadvantage. McDonald wouldn't hesitate to kill. It was there in his flat, empty eyes.

Reeves wasn't discouraged in the least. He'd pit his intelligence against blind brutality any time. And he had a chance that his captors hadn't checked his bag.

First on his plan—convince his captors to get him coffee. He would have to be at four cups, full strength to finesse his escape.

Reeves dragged his feet and staggered twice. "Tell your bosses not to give you a pharmacist job. I still see pink bunnies. Not sure how much help I can provide."

Reeves bantered, continuing his assessment of the warehouse as he was led to his room. The only exit was twenty yards from his room, a doable distance. It had the same Schlage lock. He checked for cameras, motion sensors. Two cameras were over the exit, and one over the door to his room. He didn't want to think about who else the Sureños had held in the room. He noted the smoke detectors and fire alarms on the walls and ceilings. When your shipment was worth millions of dollars, it was essential that your competition did not steal or burn your product.

Things were looking up. He was two locks and two idiots away from freedom. He had to get out of here before Galina arrived. Just the name brought up images of the Gulag and torture.

Although he didn't need to, Reeves watched McDonald enter the code again, not trusting his memory and concentration. He had never before doubted his capability. He had been identified as gifted by age five. His father was a brilliant mathematician, so it was no surprise when Reeves demonstrated the same facility. No hand-wringing or doubts in his family about what to do with the weird kid. It was accepted that he was brilliant like his esteemed father, who had been lured away from Oxford to teach at Harvard.

"Listen up. If you want me to work, I'm going to require coffee. And a lot of it. You scrambled my brains, and without caffeine, I'm no good to you."

Muscle sat on one of the chairs, his feet on the table next to Reeves's bag. "He's a real pain in the ass."

"I could go for some food. The crew should be here with the shipment soon."

McDonald was the weaker link.

"You need to eat again?"

McDonald shrugged. "Babysitting this dumb shit is boring."

Reeves had to suppress the need to retort, "You won't be bored soon."

"Once Galina gets here, you can go. But not for long. Grab it and get back here before the crew arrives. Ramirez won't be happy if you're not here when the shipment arrives."

"I'd like the French dark roast if you're going to Easy Brew." Reeves hoped McDonald would give him a clue how far he was from Palo Alto. He could be in San Diego or, God save him, in Tijuana for all he knew. A shiver of apprehension slithered down his spine. He decided not to calculate the probability of his escape. He would never admit it aloud to anyone, but sometimes the numbers lied—only because the human factor was hard to calculate. And Darcy and the Jenkinses would go against all the odds to save him. He had that much faith in them. Of course, they were missing his skills in narrowing down the search, but Izzy was no doubt coming to the rescue.

Reeves lifted a chair and took it to the other side of the table, not wanting to sit next to Muscle. He needed to prevent Muscles from spotting the Glock if it were still in his bag. He thought the chances were close to zero that these guys hadn't searched the bag. Knowing firepower, how to restrain and harm people, and how to kidnap was Gangbangers 101.

"Do we know when this Galina is going to arrive? And since when do the Sureños take orders from the Russian mob?" Reeves kept talking as he unbuckled the bag. "What's so special about Galina?"

"Don't touch your bag until Galina gets here."

"Why not? It's my bag, and you guys already opened it?"

"If you're thinking of shooting your way out of here, forget it. And thanks for the upgrade." Muscle pulled Reeves's gun from the back of his jeans.

After his sister's life had been in danger, Reeves had focused on honing his ability to defend himself and the people he cared about. But he never considered it would be necessary since the Jenkinses stood between him and the bad guys. Now, he was on his own. And he would do what he had to—avenge Tex and get more time with Darcy. He wasn't losing his chance with her without a fight.

"Leave the bag alone. You're only to access your computer when Galina is here."

Scratch plan A. But Reeves was persistent and solving the most difficult problems was his forte. Strategically, he should wait until McDonald left to even the odds. He had to assume that Galina was an SVR agent trained in torture and assassination. He would need to get close to her to immobilize her, but what to do with an armed Muscle? The alternative was torture and death. Analysis could only get you so far. It all came down to the right opportunity.

He had to escape before they got to the torture. He had a high pain tolerance, but he'd rather skip the whole experience. He assumed she was going to make him give her the unique coding that they used to develop the game. Whoever was running this operation seemed to think Reeves needed his computer to access the files. Not sure if he saw the logic in this line of reasoning. If they planned to "extract" the code, why couldn't he use any computer?

And when he didn't give up the codes, the fun would begin. He wished he had a reason why their game, out of the hundreds of thousands of games, was singled out?

Muscle's phone beeped. "She's here."

Reeves's heart rate was off to the races. He stood, not wanting to give Galina any advantage. All his childhood chess tournaments were paying off for psyching out an opponent.

Expecting Natasha, a sleek Russian villain with harsh features from the *Rocky and Bullwinkle Show*, Reeves was shocked by his nemesis's appearance. Galina, an overweight, thirty-something woman with mousy hair and horn-rimmed glasses that were sliding down her nose, wore a denim jacket and a *Game of Thrones* backpack.

"What took you so long?" Reeves crossed his arms over his chest. He had learned to take the offensive right at the beginning of a meeting from Richard Dean.

Galina blinked. Her wide-rim glasses made her look like a baby owl. "You have somewhere to go, Mr. Hewitt?"

She had no Russian accent and was dressed as if she belonged at a con of some sort.

Reeves shrugged.

"Fine, let's get started. Give me your computer and the password."

McDonald spoke to Muscle as he moved toward the door. "I'm out of here. What do you want?"

Muscle followed McDonald to the door, his back to the room. "I'm tired of burgers. Get us some teriyaki or sushi. And get this one some coffee."

With Muscle distracted, Reeves sat and opened his bag. His computer was his only weapon. Not exactly a well-hatched plan, but desperate times called for less than brilliant moves.

Placing her PC on the table, Galina moved around the table to sit next to him. "I don't want them to hurt you. But you know from seeing your friend Thompson what happens when you don't cooperate."

Reeves spotted the grip of a handgun sticking out from her denim jacket pocket—so much for the assumption from her clothing choices that Galina was "tech only." Could he be fast enough to grab the gun from a Russian agent before Muscle reacted? Anxiety and fear worked as well as caffeine. Scenarios were rapidly firing as he sorted through the probability of which one had the best chance of a non-dead, non-shot-to-the-head outcome.

"Why don't I sign in for you? It will make it a lot quicker. And you won't need to spend hours trying to get in."

"Just like that, you're going to sign in for me?" She'd never get into anything important, not even the game files. All his work was encrypted and encrypted again in his "special" way. A fake login would nuke this computer and set up a help call. And in case his escape failed, he had already overwritten the code in his files to prevent anyone from accessing the game. He'd made the changes on their flight to Santa Barbara while Darcy slept.

"Maybe. Are you sure that *Snakes Ahead* doesn't have open source code?"

Galina pushed her glasses back on her nose. "Think you're so clever. Not when they break your fingers one at a time. You'll download the code."

"That seems counterintuitive to get what you need."

Reeves's fingers were flying over the keyboard. She watched his screen. "We updated the graphics not too long ago with C++unreal. Are you familiar with the coding? Or are you more of a GC# kind of girl?"

He hoped the damn CIA and Izzy were tracking all sign-ins for the game before he made his getaway. He might make it out of the building alive, but it got more complicated and a lot dicier if he were in Tijuana.

His heart thumped against his chest, and his stomach churned like a wind turbine. He opened *Snakes Ahead* and typed in "XChoco" as the player.

"I want to show you what a difference C++unreal made to the graphics. Look closely. Do you see how well we've done with the GPUs? It's hard to appreciate since you haven't seen the old version, have you?"

She leaned forward, unable to not look like any gamer/geek. Her gun was within his grasp. It was now or torture.

"Close down the game and open your files, or he'll break your thumb."

He hesitated, pretending to decide. "I thought you'd appreciate the graphics."

With a loud, dramatic sigh, he slowly closed the game. With his left hand, he lifted the PC and slammed it with full force into her face. Her head snapped back. He hadn't knocked her out, but he was able to stun her, giving him time to grab her gun.

Muscle reached, but Reeves already had her Russian-made GSh-18 pressed against Galina's temple. "Give me a reason to fire this baby. I should blast you for what you did to my friend and the CIA agent."

Galina's nose was broken from the amount of blood gushing, and her glasses had fallen onto the table. Reeves yanked her upright by the arm, never losing sight of Muscle. "Slide your gun on the floor nice and easy toward me."

"Go ahead, shoot her. I don't give a fuck."

"You might not. But your boss and the Russians will definitely care if she dies."

Muscle slowly bent and kicked the Glock to Reeves.

Galina tried to pull away by trying to get traction for a counter move, but he wrapped his arm around her throat, cutting off her airflow. Reeves would love the chance to demonstrate his martial arts skills, in which he had the most extensive training and a lot more confidence than defending himself with a 9mm revolver.

He pushed the muzzle hard against her head. "My finger is on the trigger. Any fast movement and you're dead, your brains all over the room."

"Now, your phone." He turned to Muscle. Survival instincts blasted through him, ready to take on any threat.

Bending for the phone and keeping cover on both Galina and Muscle was a risk. This was the time for Galina to demonstrate her Russian operative skills or for Muscle to rush him.

She stiffened but didn't react when he secured both the gun and phone. Spending years gaming and typing made him quite ambidextrous, or maybe it was the "piss your pants" fear.

He tucked the Glock into his waistband and the phone into his shirt pocket. He left her phone on the table. Muscle wouldn't get past Galina's phone password.

"Hey genius, how do you plan to get out of this room?"

Reeves dragged Galina to the door, keeping his hold tight. "Enter 654123. And no fucking around. I haven't forgotten Tex."

She entered the code, and the door clicked.

He scanned the warehouse before dragging Galina out of the room. Anticipating her to make her move in the larger space, he tightened his hold on her throat, letting her feel his strength and keeping her light-headed. With the adrenaline pouring into his body, he was hyper-focused on both Muscle and Galina. Every cell was firing, aware of every shift in her body. He waited for her counterattack. Her breathing was choppy, and her body trembled. Was she that skilled to feign fear?

"Asshole, you'll be back in this room in less than five minutes, and then you're going to pay. The crew is outside. I won't go easy on you as I did with Thompson," Muscle said.

Reeves's intense training kicked in his muscle memory. His hand was steady, his body primed to react, and his heart rate was slowing. He hauled her across the room with her spine forced against his chest. The gun never wavered from her temple. Muscle hadn't rushed him, not taking the risk of Galina getting caught in the crossfire. It showed strategic thinking that Reeves didn't think the criminal was capable of.

Or maybe Muscle was covering his ass not to get killed since he either expected McDonald back or the crew was really outside the warehouse door.

Reeves tightened his forearm on Galina's windpipe. "How many guards are there waiting for me?"

She choked and gasped. Her body slackened.

"Don't think of lying to me. I've nothing to lose here, and you have a lot to lose."

He lessened his hold. She sucked air into her lungs. "None. They're picking up a shipment."

"Enter the code 654123. Now."

Reeves didn't believe her. He was a highly valued target. The Sureños surely had more than three armed guards in their "safe" warehouse if Reeves included Galina as part of the security detail.

He pushed her out the door, hyped for the next fight, but there was nothing. Nothing but old buildings. No cars. No activity. No men with assault rifles to take him back.

He scanned the area. His pounding heart lodged in his throat. The rundown warehouse was in the middle of a row of dilapidated houses and vacant office buildings. He had no idea where he was. An area of Palo Alto that he didn't know from his days at Stanford.

A busy thoroughfare was straight ahead that he'd avoid, expecting where the reinforcements would arrive from once they learned of his escape.

With full momentum, he slammed the pistol into the side of Galina's head. She'd have one helluva a headache, but she would survive—unlike Tex. She crumpled from the blow. He lowered her to the ground.

And then he ran…

CHAPTER FIFTEEN

Rubbing her eyes, trying to stay focused on the monitor, Darcy scanned the street cams at the intersection where she had been T-boned, looking at the different views of the driver to get an angle that she could run face rec on. Staring at a monitor wasn't helping her violent headache and typing with one finger wasn't helping her frustration. The FBI, CIA, and NSA teams, all better-equipped and skilled, were reviewing the same footage that she was. She should lay down to reserve her strength until they were ready to roll, but the idea of being still, allowing her mind to take over…

If she weren't busted up, she would have taken a run or hit the gym. She had to stay busy, not go down the black hole of imagining Reeves in the hands of the drug gang. From her time in Afghanistan and with the CIA, she had a lot of close-up experience to conjure up images of the lowest denominator of humankind.

Desperation swirled so close to the surface that she didn't know how to handle the feelings. It would be easier if she were the one kidnapped. She was trained in SERE—unlike Reeves. Being helpless, not able to act was worse than any torture the Sureños could cook up for her. Knowing she was responsible for Reeves's suffering, raw, primitive fear squeezed her chest in a steel vise. She had put assets in danger without this gut-wrenching worry. The assets knew the risk and had their reasons for their role. But Reeves had done nothing. And he would be safe in Seattle if she hadn't involved him. And it would have been better for him if he never met her—never agreed to work with her.

"When is the last time you took your pain pills?"

Darcy startled, unaware of Nick Jenkins's presence. It irritated her that she had missed the approach of a large man who was not trying to hide his movement.

"I never pegged you as a mom-type."

Nick ran his hand through his thick hair. "When our dad died in Iraq, I inherited the role of parenting my hell-bent brothers. There weren't many days when one of the Jenkins boys wasn't injured from pushing the limits. I had to grow up fast."

She hadn't pegged him as a man to share either. She had never thought about the cost that her brother Mike paid by being forced into the role of head of the family.

"My oldest brother was my rock after our dad was killed. He was the one who helped me get my head screwed on right by enlisting. From what I've read and heard about the Jenkins brothers, it looks like you did a good job too."

She and Nick had one thing in common: neither liked receiving praise for doing their job.

"You should take a break. You'll do Reeves no good…"

Cutting too close to the truth, Darcy snapped, "Sure, I'll go take a nap, maybe take a hot bath. That will really help."

"Take a break, soldier. It isn't a choice."

He was a big man who was trying to intimidate her, but his intentions were honorable. She had to remind herself that he wasn't the enemy, but right now, she needed a punching bag. And Nick Jenkins looked as if he could handle whatever she threw at him.

"I'm in charge, and I'll take a break when we have actionable intel. And not before."

"Suit yourself, but I'm in charge of the assault. And I won't take a team member who is a risk to herself and my team." He emphasized "my" with his deep voice.

She should be thanking Nick—for allowing her, injured as she was, to be part of the team to recover Reeves. Nick didn't do it because she was charming or compliant or was as skilled as him. She was sure it was because of Nick's regards for Reeves. For a reason she couldn't comprehend, Nick believed Reeves cared about her and would want her there when he came out.

She pushed herself up from the chair with one hand and faced him. "I can't do nothing."

"I get it, but you've got to trust the team. Everyone is working their asses off to find something. Izzy is using some secret NSA software to find which of the hundred cars left the parking garage in the time frame when they transferred Reeves from the ambulance. And Molly is monitoring all the traffic out of Palo Alto, airports, bus stations, and gas station cameras. Every possibility of how and where they transported Reeves. NSA and CIA and FBI are using their superpowers to find him. And then when they get us the intel, we'll go in. And I need you to be in good shape, or Reeves will threaten to kick my ass again."

Black humor was standard practice among military types for coping with high-risk threats. Darcy wasn't prepared for the effect serious and grim Nick Jenkins's attempt to make her laugh in the middle of a shitstorm had on her.

Tears welled behind her eyes. She covered her mouth with her hand, trying to hold in all the fear and pain. She never cried. Not since her father had been killed. She swallowed hard and brushed at the tears, hoping to hell that Nick wouldn't try to console her.

"Any word from the FBI on Ramirez yet?"

Darcy's respect for Nick Jenkins grew exponentially. She was grateful that he hadn't offered any comfort.

"Nothing from the FBI yet. It will take time—time we don't have." Darcy tried to bring her hands together and was stopped by the damn sling.

When Darcy had contacted the FBI, the conversation immediately became a pissing match since kidnapping fell into the FBI purview. But after a phone call between her boss and the FBI director, the CIA was still in the lead. From their ongoing investigation into organized crime, the FBI identified Raoul Ramirez as one of Sureños's lieutenants working in Palo Alto. The

FBI was running everything on him and all his associates—credit cards, travel, bank accounts—to find where he did his business.

"The Palo Alto Police Department's gang unit wasn't useful. Nothing that we didn't already know. Of course, the police chief wanted to send SWAT helicopters to search all the industrial areas. The chief is jumping at the chance to use his SWAT team since they don't see a lot of action. The FBI nixed the locals from alerting the kidnappers into acting rashly."

Nick paced, running his hand through his hair, a tell of his stress. Like Darcy, he hated sitting around. "Anything from the Sureños CI in Santa Barbara?"

Every agency was doing their thing, but it wasn't enough—every time she thought of Reeves, she couldn't breathe, couldn't concentrate.

"I think he's our best bet for information on what warehouses they use along the coast to ship between Mexico and the rest of the states. The detective who handles him sent the message to make contact, but it could be hours or even days before the CI can communicate. He can't just break his cover and disappear to contact his handle."

Darcy was well-versed in all the ways connecting with an asset could go wrong. Her CIA heart told her that the CI might be the break they needed. If he was able to get away from the gang.

"What the hell?" Nick rushed away to the sound of a woman's voice. "How the fuck did they get here?"

Darcy followed Nick toward the entrance of the house but lagged behind, not knowing what to expect. Had Reeves's sister arrived? Nick wouldn't bring her here, would he? Anxiety about meeting Emily, whom Reeves deeply cared about, made her more off-kilter than should be possible right now when her world was twirling. How could she explain to his sister that it was her operation that put Reeves in harm's way?

Two blondes—one tall and svelte, and the other with curves, both dressed very fashionably—breezed through the highly secure front door. Darcy recognized Sophie Dean from the picture, and she was more gorgeous in person. Her blonde curls were cut in a style that framed her face versus Darcy's out-of-control Orphan Annie look. Darcy patted her hair, trying to tame it. She had lost her clip somewhere along the way, and her hair required two hands to control. Her appearance was the least of her present concerns.

Lars came from the back room where he was putting together the team's equipment. His chin was thrust forward, his shoulders tight at the sight of the women. "What the hell are you doing here? I thought we agreed you'd stay in Seattle?"

"And I missed you too." The tall woman had to be Danni Knorr. She matched the CIA description of the woman who the Triad had kidnapped with Jordan and Sophie Dean, and was now in an obvious relationship with Lars Jenkins.

"Sophie, you didn't clear this with Finn, did you?"

"FYI, Nick, I don't have to clear with Finn a trip to help a friend."

"And how do you plan to help Reeves? Huh?" Nick's face tightened in a severe grimace. "You have all the latest intel as it comes in. How does coming here change anything except you getting in the way?"

"Lars, tell Sophie where Finn is while Nick cools off." Danni rubbed Lars's chest and snuggled close to him.

"Sophie, Finn is coordinating with the FBI's HRT team for the rescue. He won't be back for several hours."

"Perfect. That gives us time." Sophie grinned at Nick, oblivious to the two-hundred-pounds of seething male rage.

"I'm in charge here and not Finn, so don't think you'll convince me to change my mind." Nick used his commander's voice.

"Whoa, Nick, take a breath," Danni said. "The house is large enough to hold a full battalion, and neither of us is planning to interfere. We're here to help everyone handle the stress."

"This isn't a social event. We all have to be on our A game. Not distracted or entertained." Nick's face was beet red. The muscles in his neck strained. His carotids visibly pulsated.

Sophie wrapped her arms around Nick and hugged him. "We're worried too. We couldn't stay away. We needed to be together."

Surprisingly, Nick hugged her tightly back. "I need to get him back before Emily finds out. She'll be devastated."

Darcy was shocked by the grim ex-Marine captain's frank admission of concern for Reeves's sister. He trusted Sophie Dean with his feelings. And then Darcy remembered that the Dean sisters had grown up with the Jenkins brothers. They were family, and as Nick had told her, they all considered Reeves part of that family. Suddenly, she felt like an interloper and backed up to sneak away from emotional entanglement, which she excelled at. Losing both her parents, she had resolved never to get too close. Involvement meant loss and gut-wrenching grief.

Danni released Lars and skewered Darcy with a whole-body perusal. Her expressive eyes tracked up and down Darcy's person. "Not so fast. We have a lot to talk about."

Darcy never ran from a fight. But right now, she wanted to run as fast as she could. She played no part in this touching scene with everyone who cared about Reeves when there was nothing between them except for the flaming lust. She marched into the foyer where they were huddled, her flip-flops slapping against the marble entry.

Sophie's eyes softened in sympathy. "You poor thing."

Not now, please not now, no kindness when her guard was down. Darcy didn't want to face these sophisticated women who were important to Reeves.

Danni moved right into Darcy's space. "My God, it's good we came." She put her hand on her hip and glared at Lars and Nick. "You let that poor woman stay in her bloody skirt."

Darcy had done her homework on all of Reeves's friends, looking for connections to terrorists. Danni had gone to MIT and was another of Reeves's circle of brilliant and beautiful women. Had Danni or Sophie been one of Reeves's friends with benefits? Darcy's face heated with embarrassment. Reeves was missing, and she was jealous of the women in his life? Her concussion had scrambled her brains. She didn't want to admit that Reeves Hewitt had done more to her with one kiss than any blow to her head.

"I'm fine. Thank you." Could she turn any redder under both women's intense scrutiny?

"You're not fine. You have one arm in a sling and no one to help you. When Lars and I were working together on a case, I was almost run over by a van and broke my arm."

Lars coughed dramatically.

Danni whipped around, her hand back on her hip. "We only worked together once you accepted that I could be of help."

"Yes, honey." Lars winked at her.

"I was in a splint for weeks. Trust me, I haven't forgotten how difficult it was to accomplish basic life functions. I had Lars to help me. But you have no one until the Jenkins brothers bring Reeves back. They will. You needn't worry. They never accept failure. It was probably tattooed on their butts when they were born."

Darcy appreciated any woman who had no qualms standing up to alpha males. She and Danni had a lot in common—except for style, looks, and brains.

"My clothes won't fit you, but Sophie's will."

Danni was back to perusing Darcy's body. Her eyes took in every inch of Darcy's chest and her curvy hips and bottom. "You can't be comfortable in that skirt."

"I have yoga pants that will fit. And you'll be able to move more comfortably. But I'm not sure about the top." Sophie moved to stand next to Danni.

Darcy winced with their blunt assessment but refused to be intimidated. She had stood up to a lot worse inspection by the brass. Although Sophie had a similarly curvy body, Darcy's chest was much larger.

"Will it hurt too much to change your shirt?" Danni asked.

"I have a soft cotton long sleeve shirt that will make you look more professional. Handling all these men, you have to be at your best. I wish it weren't so, but that's the reality of our world."

Sophie wasn't judging Darcy's body but assessing how to make her more comfortable. Darcy flashed on how difficult it had been to pull her panties down to use the facility. Not that she wanted the women's help.

Losing the braless t-shirt look was appealing. Eventually, she would be interacting with the FBI and local police, and it was difficult enough to assert her authority, being female and height challenged. Going braless wasn't ideal when working with men.

"Don't try to fight them, Darcy. You won't win." Lars's intimate look at Danni was telling.

"You like it when you lose, Lars," Danni countered with an infectious grin.

"We understand you have CIA business. Unless you have something to do right now, let Danni, and I give you a little sisterly TLC. We're very good at that." Sophie was encouraging and sweet.

"And we have a lot to share about Reeves. You want to hear everything, don't you?" Danni raised her perfectly shaped eyebrows.

Darcy would like to get out of the bloody skirt and definitely would like to have a bra for taking down the Sureños. But it meant asking one of the women to help her. She needed to woman up. Utilizing available resources on a mission was part of adapting to the circumstances. And Danni and Sophie were concerned and caring resources.

"Reeves is the son my father always wanted. He told us that Reeves was speechless upon meeting you. Reeves is never speechless." Sophie's blue eyes were like the crystalline mountain lakes in Pakistan's Karakoram range. One of Darcy's better memories during her deployment.

"Listening to all our stories will help distract you until there is news." Danni took her arm to lead Darcy away. "And you'll be doing us a favor. Helping you means we're taking care of Reeves. And getting to talk about our dear friend will lessen our worry. You wouldn't say no, would you? A woman who shut up Reeves must be very special."

Darcy wanted to protest that Reeves wasn't enthralled, but she didn't get a chance.

"And we're dying to tell you about Lily, his ex, who we all despised."

And with the promise of information about Lily, Darcy was hooked. She was a CIA officer whose business was information. And Darcy should have known not to underestimate Danni. The gorgeous woman wasn't the fluff she appeared to be. Not everyone graduated from MIT.

"Danni, Reeves won't like you butting into his business, especially when he isn't here to defend himself," Lars said.

"Now, whose fault is it that Reeves isn't here? It's time for the Jenkins brothers to do their magic."

"Never doubt it, honey. We'll find him," Lars said.

"Darcy needs to rest and eat. She was assaulted and T-boned in the last six hours. Cut the romance talk and get her to lie down," Nick ordered.

"Of course, Nick," Sophie intoned in the sweetest voice.

"Does that work with Finn?" Nick asked.

"Yes. He likes when I'm all agreeable."

"You haven't been agreeable since you were five years old."

"Not for you, but for Finn, I am. Until I don't want to be." Sophie laughed over her shoulder.

Exhausted, Darcy couldn't fight against the tide of two strong-willed women surrounding her. She allowed herself to be led down the hall and taken in by the teasing warmth of Reeves's friends.

CHAPTER SIXTEEN

Reeves sprinted down the alley, keeping to the side, hiding in the shadows of the two-story buildings. He raced toward the fading sunlight, away from the busy thoroughfare. As he looked over his shoulder, his senses heightened, waiting for the gunshot. His heart was revving as his muscles pumped hard, pushing not to be an open target. He'd soon have the cover of darkness.

By now, Galina had probably alerted the gang. They would be combing the area, knowing he couldn't get far in his overdosed state. He had to get out of the open.

He wasn't going to last long at this pace. The adrenaline surge from his escape would only take him so far. His energy was lagging, his breathing choppy, and his legs were weakening. And his dress shoes were inhibiting his "run for your life" scenario. Under pressure, his focus jumped all over the place as he ran through mathematical outcomes based on different choices. Algorithms exploded in his brain.

He neared the far end of one of the rows of warehouses with still no one coming. Why hadn't Muscle chased him? Nothing was stopping the guy, and he was fit.

He stared out at the street in front of him, a rundown residential area with small, dilapidated houses. He had no clue about his location. Nothing looked familiar—not one landmark that he recognized. And he was too far away to read the street sign.

To get to the residential area, he'd have to be out in the open too long, giving the Sureños time to spot him. To survive, he had to find a hideout in the industrial section until the Jenkins brothers and Darcy got there.

He had to cross the alley, which required that he come out of the shadows to get to the next row. He stopped at the corner. He felt the uptick in his heartbeat when he left the relative safety of the shadows. His roaring pulse resounded in his ears. His loud gasps blasted the eerie silence. It was difficult to switch from running as fast as you could in order to avoid a bullet to slow, quiet stealth. His body was in overdrive. His sympathetic nervous system dialed up to flight mode.

He took measured breaths as he crept to the next corner. He held his breath and peered around the corner, prepared to see the armed Sureños. A forklift was parked halfway into the doorway on the opposite side as if the operator were on a break. He waited and watched, trying to ease his thumping heart rate and breathing. He saw and heard no one. His body was attuned to every sound and sight.

Reeves had to take the chance that it was empty. He could try to elicit help if people were working in the space. But that would only put innocent people in the way of the Sureños. It all depended on how many people he found in the warehouse and whether there was any chance of them taking on the armed and dangerous Sureños.

He hugged the wall of the first two buildings.

He searched for an open door where he could find cover and call Nick. He'd like to call Darcy first, but he didn't have her number memorized.

He stopped when he had a good view of the entrance into the rectangular space filled with crates. No movement and no sound. He rushed through the doorway, and once out of view, he paused to assess.

Nothing that he could detect. There were stacks of wooden boxes in the front of the forklift as if they had just been placed there. He raced to the back of the warehouse, keeping between the crates. He dialed Nick from the phone he'd taken from Muscle.

Nick immediately answered. "Nick Jenkins."

"Nick, I'm okay. Is Darcy all right?"

"Thank God." Reeves heard Nick's long exhale. "She's fine. Sitrep."

"I don't recognize the location, but I'm in an industrial area with rows of warehouses. Not sure how long before the Sureños will find me. I'm going to take out the SIM card after this call."

"Are you wounded?"

"I'm weak from the overdose but nothing else. They hadn't gotten to the torture yet. I'm hiding in the back of the second warehouse on the eastside, using the setting sun as my guide. I have no idea what row I'm in. I'm armed with a GSh-18."

"We've got you. Hang tight. You're in East Palo Alto, ten minutes out. Stay hidden, no matter what you hear. And only start shooting if you have to. No damn heroics. If anything happened to you, Emily would never forgive me."

"I love you too." Reeves shut the phone down to remove the SIM card. Ten minutes was going to be an eternity. He hadn't told Nick to tell Darcy… What could Nick tell Darcy? That Reeves loved her? It was a little premature, but he had never felt this way about a woman, and he didn't think anything could change how he felt. He had to consider if it was some sort of crazy rebound phenomenon to have this blinding attraction. Nope, he wanted Darcy as he had never wanted another woman.

His hands shook as he disabled the phone, and he was a bit dizzy. The symptoms might be dehydration or the effects of the drugs in his system. He moved to face the door, giving him a sightline on unwelcome visitors. He didn't calculate his chances with one weapon against the Sureños's heavy firepower.

He lowered himself to the floor, knowing he needed to reserve his strength for the next round. He was depleted in every way. His nerves were jacked up, but his body was weary, his mouth dry, his head throbbing. What he would do for water and Darcy right now.

He pulled out the GSh-18 to check how much ammunition Galina required to intimidate him. And how long could he last against the Sureños?

He had enough ammo to make a statement but nothing more. He refused to let them take him back. He had to hold out. Darcy waited for him.

He leaned against the crate and closed his eyes for a second. The back of his eyelids rubbed like sandpaper. He couldn't fall asleep. To do so would be fatal.

Reeves jerked awake at the sound of hushed voices. He hadn't been asleep but rather in a mediative state. He heard the slap of footsteps on the concrete floor and the click of assault rifles. The threat of an imminent attack charged his body awake with a flood of adrenaline, skyrocketing his heart rate, tightening his muscles. Sweat beaded his forehead.

He pushed up from the floor, trying not to make any sound, focused on his view. And waited as his pulse tripped into outer space. He slowed his breath and steadied his hand as he raised it into a firing position.

Nick, followed by Finn and Lars, were a welcoming sight in their vests with their assault rifles moving in formation through the space. He blinked twice to make sure they were real and not a drug hallucination.

Nick spoke into his comm mic. "We've got him. Repeat. We've got the target."

A voice Reeves didn't recognize came over Nick's mic. "The warehouse is cleared."

He had to suppress the need to hug the macho men who were bristling with aggression, still on high alert, even with their weapons now not pointed at him.

"Took you long enough, guys!" It was either be a smart-ass or weep tears of relief.

Reeves almost lost his balance when Nick slapped him hard on his back.

"Fuck, is it good to see your sorry ass!" Nick's voice cracked.

"Never thought I'd be this happy to see the Jenkins brothers." His comment got a heavy thump from Finn and a fist bump from Lars.

"Darcy, we've got him. He's upright but looks like shit."

"Darcy is here?" Reeves staggered as his stomach bottomed out. "Why in the hell would you allow her to come to a potential firefight when she's injured?"

He thought he'd have time to regroup before seeing her.

"She's been at the front entrance waiting until we cleared the building, dumb ass." Nick never reacted well when his solid judgment was questioned. Too bad. This was Darcy.

"Man, you better not let her hear you. The woman is Army and a CIA officer. She can handle herself. And you better remember that when you want to go all alpha on her, or she'll take you down. Learn from my stupid-ass mistakes with Danni. Never underestimate your woman." Lars grinned.

"Do you need help walking?" Finn's baby blues were lasered onto Reeves, seeing more than Reeves wanted the SEAL to see.

"Right, asshole. I'm fine."

And he was grateful that the Jenkins kept their comments to themselves when he stumbled before righting himself. But he didn't miss the concerned look between Nick and Finn.

Damn it. He didn't want Darcy to see him like this. He understood her over-responsible, guilty self would be upset. But he knew how to tease her out of the "weight of the world rests on my shoulders" attitude.

The promise of teasing Darcy lightened his step.

Darcy had never been this amped up. Her heart rate was in the red zone, nearing stroke level. She tried for slow, easy breaths, but she was too jacked from the adrenaline flooding her body. Not being able to rush in and defend Reeves was worse than the T-boning or the punch to the face. Hamstrung by her injuries, waiting outside as the Jenkinses and the FBI's HRT teams assaulted the warehouse was a living hell.

She was stuck in a nightmarish time warp. The seconds were measured by her frantic helplessness and the "what if" scenarios rocketing through her. Her fear exponentially grew as she waited. If they were too late…would they find Reeves as they had Tex? All that joy and life gone. His laughing eyes, his teasing banter snuffed out. Replaced with an empty, blank stare.

She shifted her weight and fought to bring herself into the moment. To keep her discipline and training at the forefront and not let her thoughts sink into a black hole. The air wouldn't move in her lungs. Finn must have tightened her Kevlar vest too tight.

Her nerves were strung taut as a piano wire ready to snap, and she was aware of the silence as the team moved through the warehouse. Radio silent. She was isolated except for two members of the HRT team next to her to protect the entrance if the Sureños arrived. And although no one said it, to cover her. She coped with her stress by getting physical, fighting the bad guys, and instead, she was trapped—unable to protect others—useless to the team.

No shots. Nothing from the warehouse. Her stomach roiled. Reeves was gone. The Sureños had arrived before the team. Raw anguish filled her chest. The Sureños would torture Reeves for escaping before they killed him. She leaned against the wall for support.

She had taken lives and caused lives to be taken in the Army and the CIA. They were bad players, and she liked to believe that her actions had saved lives. She had never harmed an innocent before. Remorse weighed on her soul. Reeves was a vibrant and caring man. The world would lose a shining light.

She would never stop looking for him. She would never give up. Resolve helped her screw her head on straight. Spinning in her thoughts, she almost missed Nick's voice.

Reeves was alive. Safe. Close by. Tears burned behind her eyes, and relief made her knees shaky. She would not cry now in front of the entire testosterone-dominated HRT team and the Jenkins brothers.

She ran to the back of the warehouse, following the sound of the voices. Darcy dodged the forklift and the HRT team that was streaming down the aisles.

One of the men pointed to the right to guide her.

She was breathless, not from the exertion, but from all the emotions bubbling that she had been holding inside—overpowering feelings that she had walled up into an impenetrable box.

"Darcy." A very pale Reeves walked toward her, listing to the left. His hair was a mess, dark circles framed his bloodshot eyes, and his dress shirt was rumpled. And he'd never looked more beautiful.

She slowed, suddenly unsure. How would she ever explain how her feelings for him had dramatically shifted in the hours that he had been missing? The woman who wasn't afraid of anything had been terrified of losing him. What if he didn't have the same extraordinary revelation?

Not pausing, he pulled her gently into his arms, wrapping her in his warmth. "I was so afraid that I'd never see you again. That my life was finished when we'd barely got started."

Darcy snuggled close, breathing in his vitality, absorbing his body heat, feeling his steady heartbeat. "I want to get started right now."

Nick's deep voice boomed in the high-ceiling space. "You should probably wait until he's had some water and has eaten."

"Or Reeves may never get started," Lars joked over his shoulder as the brothers walked away.

"They're such assholes."

"They're right." She knew she was being selfish, but she needed to hold him after all the terror. She wanted to reassure herself that he was safe and alive. "You look pretty unsteady. Do you need medical care?"

"You're not going to call another ambulance for me, are you?"

The glint in Reeves's eyes and his teasing tone made everything in Darcy's world begin to right itself.

"You're incorrigible." She gazed up, wanting to see every detail of his angular face, the beard stubble on his chin, the shape of his full lips. "My God, I want to kill those bastards."

He gently pushed her hair away from her face, tenderly outlining with his fingertip the bruising on her cheek and then her swollen lips.

"Looks like we'll both have to recover before I can kiss you the way I want to." He bent and touched his warm lips to hers. "I never want you to have another moment of pain. I've never experienced icy fear as when the bastard bragged about hurting you. Not knowing how badly you were injured was worse than any torture they could have inflicted on me."

Darcy absorbed his every word, trying to believe, to accept that this wonderful man shared the same feelings. How could the dark, sinister world she inhabited bring such joy into her life? She didn't care how they came together. They were together. And she'd fight to keep them that way.

"Watching your convulsions was the same—primitive terror. One minute you were carefree and laughing, and then when I learned that you had been overdosed…" Her body pressed against his. She might never let him go. "I should have never involved you once I knew you were innocent."

He rubbed her back in soothing circles, allowing her to vent her guilt.

"If you hadn't come with me to California, you'd still be safe in Seattle, working on the ransomware."

He scattered kisses along her hairline, across her forehead. She was losing steam from his gentleness.

He lifted her chin and looked directly into her eyes. His tone was serious, his eyes without any amusement. "You couldn't have stopped me from coming. I would have followed you. And imagine what trouble I would have gotten into without my CIA watchdog."

She laughed and cried at the same time, a jumble of emotions. "I hate when you do that."

"Do what?" He waggled his eyebrows. "Leave you breathless with my charm and wit?"

"Make me laugh. Make me realize that there is more to living than catching bad guys."

"Is this what I think it means?" He pressed kisses to her palm, making her skin hot and her stomach twirl. "You care about me, Darcy Wilson. It only took me being kidnapped for you to realize it."

"I do care about you, you insufferable jerk. Do you have to gloat?"

"I'm not gloating. I'm ecstatic. I've fled torture to be in the arms of the bravest and most beautiful woman with the finest ass on the planet." He squeezed her ass in his big hands. "These babies made escaping so sweet."

His pleasure in touching her gutted her. No one ever made her feel needed; no one made her feel wanted for herself—a curvy, bad-ass CIA officer.

"When did the CIA mandate skin-tight pants as part of the uniform? Lucky I was rescued. With all the men watching this delicious behind instead of kicking down the door, I'm amazed they made it into the warehouse."

"Except the door was wide open." Darcy pushed against his hardness, pleasure blossoming under her skin. A weak but virile Reeves still got her going.

"Smart-ass. You've interrupted my ode to your body. I can't decide what I like most, your freckles scattered across your nose"—he kissed her bruised and swollen nose—"or the mole next to your lip, right here." He gently touched the spot before he kissed it. "Or this." He squeezed her butt. "Being held captive helps put your life into perspective. My life goal is to worship you, so you never doubt what a magnificent woman you are in this incredible little package."

Her stomach fluttered and flitted like birds in a summer breeze. Was Reeves serious, or was this the adrenaline and the desperation to grab onto life after being at death's door? She didn't care what the reasons were. She was trained to trust her gut. And this was genuine.

"I feel like a new man. Who needs water and rest when you have tough and gorgeous Darcy Wilson caring for you?"

"Let's go, Reeves," Finn shouted. "Have you molested that woman enough yet?"

"I haven't even started," Reeves yelled back, which was followed by loud laughs.

Taking her hand into his, he whispered near her ear, "I plan to never stop."

And Darcy swayed into his side, dizzy with need. His deep voice and the promise in his eyes heated her blood.

CHAPTER SEVENTEEN

Reeves half-listened to the Jenkins boys trash talk in the safe house's living room after their debrief. His focus was on Darcy, who was across the room with the women—too far from him, too far to touch. She tried to smile when Danni clinked their champagne glasses together. With her face swollen, and her arm back in the splint, she had to be hurting and irritated by the limitations of having her arm pinned to her side. He had plans to help with her frustration once they ditched the friends.

Sophie and Danni were on either side of Darcy, chatting away as if they were longtime friends. At one point, Sophie adjusted the sling on Darcy's shoulder. Interesting that his fiercely independent CIA agent smiled at Sophie's ministrations. He still was a bit in shock that Darcy had succumbed to the women who were like a tsunami, swallowing you up in their care and concern. He would have thought that uptight Darcy would avoid being swept into his friend group. She wasn't buttoned-up now in a black, clingy dress that hugged every one of her luscious curves—curves that he was dying to explore. This looked like the work of Danni and Sophie for the sole reason of watching him lose his sanity.

He swallowed hard, fighting his emotional response to how his close friends had welcomed Darcy. He hadn't realized until now the women had never made any effort to include Lily. Why hadn't he noticed? Because he had been working nonstop. He had been essential to the rescue of the Dean sisters, Danni, and his sister.

Lily played no role in that all-consuming part of his life. And it was telling that he never considered including her.

He always thought that Lily wasn't accepted because she was a tech geek and didn't have anything in common with the women. But CIA Darcy was the polar opposite of Sophie and Danni, and they were laughing together like best buds. And Izzy slipped into their group whenever she made it back to town.

His fierce hunger for Darcy must have telegraphed across the living room since she glanced up. Their eyes locked. He couldn't control the raging need for this one woman who knocked his life off its axis. The connection arcing between them was kinetic, rearranging the molecules in the air around them, forming their own force field. He needed her now. Darcy's face and chest reddened before she looked down, nodding to something an animated Sophie was saying.

There was no logic to his need for this woman. There were no algorithms or formulas for blind attraction. And seeing his friend's acceptance of Darcy made it feel right.

But what would Darcy think? She was committed to her work with the CIA, which meant foreign assignments far away from Seattle. And he and the CIA hierarchy would never be friends. After his in-your-face experience with the Sureños, he was more dedicated than ever to working with cyber-security. No one should have to suffer as he had—drugged/overdosed with convulsions. He wanted to stop every asshole. He had the skills the good guys needed.

Finn raised his beer. "To Reeves. For proving that he is truly a Jenkins with his sheer courage in rigging his escape."

The women joined the circle and raised their glasses. After the overdose of drugs, Reeves was limiting himself to water. He raised his water bottle and met Darcy's warm gaze.

He was still on emotional overload. The relief of his escape, Finn the Navy SEAL acknowledging him as one of the Jenkins brotherhood, and Darcy's declaration had him whirling. He couldn't lose it now when the macho men had brought him into their fold. The Jenkins smart-asses would never allow him to live it down if he got sappy.

He never wavered in his gaze at Darcy. "When I was locked in the room, I never doubted for a minute that you would find me, would never fail, never stop until I was rescued because of your deep commitment." His voice cracked. "And I was one damn lucky man to have the best looking for me."

Reeves meant the words for Darcy and, from the way that her lips parted and her skin flushed a pretty pink, she knew it too.

"Here, here." And everyone raised their glasses.

Before anyone had finished swallowing, Danni announced, "I want revenge on the bastards who dared to hurt Darcy and Reeves." Danni's eyes narrowed before she put her hand on her hip and glared at Nick. "What's the plan?"

Lars put his arm around Danni's shoulder, pulling her next to him. "That's my girl."

Smiling, Darcy spoke directly to Danni. "I appreciate and second the sentiment heartily. I want to put the scum behind bars for overdosing Reeves. We're waiting on intel before we can act. Molly and Izzy both are trying to crack the phone that Reeves retrieved from the Sureños gangbanger. They're also searching through every database to find the Russian Galina. They'll get back to me as soon as they get a hit. It shouldn't be too much longer."

"I want to use my Krav Maga on the animal who punches a woman in the face," Danni said matter-of-factly.

Lars chuckled. "Down, tiger. Remember your promise."

Reeves loved Danni for her passionate need to defend Darcy. But he didn't want Danni near the vicious gang. He didn't want Darcy near them either. But he couldn't stop her. He had to either respect her abilities or walk away. He knew it was a game-changer in their relationship. It would be like her asking him to give up his tech life.

"I called the detective in Santa Barbara who is running the CI in the Sureños. It didn't add up that the gang didn't come after Reeves once he escaped."

"They were too scared once they witnessed my superpowers, honey." He loved how quickly her skin took on a rosy glow, and her lips pressed tightly together. She wasn't a CIA officer for nothing. She read his intention with the promise of his superpowers all focused on her. And when it came to his need for Darcy, he just might have superpowers.

The Jenkins hooted loudly. Sophie rolled her eyes, and Danni winked at him.

Darcy cleared her throat. "As I was saying."

God, he was getting a boner from her prim, first grade teacher tone.

"The CI made contact, and the word is the Sureños have backed out of a big deal. It seems the Sureños have an informant in the FBI who warned them that every alphabet agency was looking for them. And the Sureños, good businessmen that they are, after learning how hard the hammer would fall on their drug trade, backed off."

Admiration for his woman filled him. After the hours of "debriefing" by Nick and Darcy, he had crashed. They fed him and gave him water while they asked endless questions. And when he thought he was done, they'd start again. He understood their reasoning to ask the questions immediately while it was fresh, before he forgot any details.

He did enjoy the shocked look on both Darcy and Nick's faces when he described his escape. Nick had sworn him to secrecy to never retell the risks to Emily. Reeves planned to use his new incentive in creative ways on Nick.

Darcy had gone pale and silent. He tried to reassure her, but he hadn't succeeded. She barely uttered a word during his description, promising that they would discuss it further when alone. He looked forward to her passionate reprimand. He had hoped to spend his first hours out of captivity naked with Darcy. Instead, he slept for hours while she was doing her CIA shtick. It seemed convulsions and cocaine tired even fast-firing brains.

"We need the link between the Sureños and the Russians." Reeves was clearheaded now. And he needed to get back in the game. He should be offended that they hadn't asked him to run the phone and Galina, but he accepted Darcy's demand that he rest, or he would be of no value to the team when they really needed him. He did make her promise if he rested that she would join him in bed tonight. Win-win for him.

"Once we're finished here, I'll have Molly and Izzy bring me up to speed."

"I was about to tell the group before Danni made her sentiments loud and clear." Nick gave Danni his "I'm in charge" look, which never had any effect on Danni. Especially since Danni and Emily had become very close, and Nick would pay if he mistreated Emily's friend.

"I wasn't loud, just succinct in my need for bloody revenge."

Nick shook his head. "Richard called me a few minutes ago after speaking with the CIA director. The ransomware hackers have placed the embassy information for sale on the dark web. Now the focus is how to trap who is behind the sale."

Reeves moved to be next to Darcy, knowing that she would be upset that she hadn't yet received the information before Richard. "Honey, it's not personal. It's the politics of how these government agencies run. Richard is very close to the president and his chief of staff."

"How can I be effective if Dean is getting information before I am?"

"Yeah, it sucks. Bureaucracies just work that way."

Her phone, which she'd tucked into her sling, buzzed right on cue. "It's the director. I need to take this." She didn't look at anyone but walked toward the French doors to the deck.

CHAPTER EIGHTEEN

Reeves only heard "Yes, sir" before Darcy walked onto the deck. He looked at Nick. "Do you have any idea what's going on? Did Richard mention anything?"

Nick shrugged. "I might have put a bug in Richard's ear about Wilson's outstanding performance and suggested that we were interested in hiring her."

Reeves grinned. "Nice thinking. Good to know that you're more than a pretty face."

His mind exploded with the possibilities of sharing their work and life. Would Darcy even consider leaving the CIA to join Jenkins Security? It was a real stretch and not the kind of career decision a careful woman like Darcy would make without time and space. She wouldn't want to be pushed.

"Very funny, jackass," Nick countered.

"Now that he's a brother, we get to hit him, right, Nick?" Lars deadpanned.

"No marks. Emily would be upset."

Reeves spaced out on the Jenkinses ragging on each other and watched Darcy through the glass windows. She paced, allowing brief glimpses of her pert profile with her hair clipped back. She wasn't doing much of the talking, and he couldn't tell by her body language whether she was receiving kudos or being reprimanded. It was going to be almost impossible to withhold his opinion on the treatment she received at the hands of the CIA if she had been criticized over his kidnapping.

Absorbed with Darcy, Reeves missed the moment when the subject turned to weddings. Everyone was in the "engaged and planning" stages of their weddings. At one point, Reeves had suggested to Danni and Sophie having one big Jenkins bash. His suggestion was met with absolute horror by the women. Not one would consider the logic of the idea.

Darcy had ended her call and walked into the room. Her lips were not locked shut. That was a good sign, wasn't it? Except for the enigmatic look that he couldn't read.

"Any news, Darcy?" Sensitive to others, Sophie had noted the change in Darcy's demeanor.

"Nothing on the case. I'm a little stunned. The director basically offered me the assignment in Libya that I've always wanted after Richard Dean mentioned that he was interested in offering me a job. Was that your idea, Nick?"

"It never hurts for the boss to hear how good his underlings are doing."

"Thanks. It's my dream station."

"Why Libya? It's not a friendly place for women." Sophie had a global foundation supporting refugee women and was very knowledgeable about the issues women faced in various countries.

"It would be incredibly challenging. The Russians and the Chinese are hiding behind humanitarian works as they infiltrate the infrastructure to control Libya's resources and be strategically placed in Africa. American intelligence is vital to our long-term presence and to prevent Russian and Chinese dominance."

Libya. Reeves reeled as if he had been gut-punched. Always quick with words, at this moment, Reeves had none. No witty rejoinder.

Danni moved closer to Reeves in a show of support. "Libya? I guess Reeves can wrack up a lot of airline miles. He can work anywhere as long as there is a Wi-Fi connection."

Danni's attempt at humor fell flat.

Nick shrugged and shook his head. "Didn't see that coming."

Darcy didn't cross the room to stand by him but positioned herself next to Nick. Already distancing herself. And what of her earlier promises? The ground was unsteady under him as if he were mired in quicksand. His words came out wooden. "That's great, Darcy. Sounds like quite an adventure."

What of their adventures?

His phone rang, stopping his friends from watching as his heart was ripped out of his chest.

"Reeves, I thought you were tech support. How did you get yourself kidnapped?" It was an ongoing joke between Izzy and him. It was their standard cover when explaining their work to avoid acknowledging their role in cybersecurity.

"I didn't 'get myself kidnapped.' It sounds like you've been listening to the Jenkins gossip."

"Put your phone on speaker so everyone can hear," Izzy demanded.

Reeves pressed the speaker button. "You're now speaking to Nick, Finn, Lars, Danni, Sophie, and Darcy."

He knew it was childish to place Darcy last. But she had crashed his bright new world. And it would take him time to adjust.

"Listen up. I performed my magic on the phone Reeves purloined from our gangbanger. Do you want to hear how I did it, Reeves?"

Reeves laughed, but the sound was hollow. "I already know, but maybe the Jenkins would want to hear. They are always interested in tech explanations...not."

"I should sucker punch you. You always want to explain when we're in the middle of an operation," Finn said.

"Prepare yourself, Reeves. Nothing I have to report is good. Charlie Poll is dead. His body was found a week ago, washed up on a beach in San Diego. The reported cause of death was an overdose of cocaine and Xanax."

"How can you be sure it's Charlie?" Darcy asked.

"We were able to track the phone calls that the kidnapper made in the last two days. I'm sorry, Reeves, but the calls were to Professor Wainwright."

Izzy paused, waiting for his reaction.

"Go on, Izzy. Nothing will surprise me today." So, he sounded bitter. Nothing like getting kicked when you were already down on the ground.

"Once we connected Wainwright with the gang member, we ran his phone. He used the phone only to call two numbers—the Sureños, and the other number we tracked to San Diego and to a man named Alan Turing. It didn't take much to connect the dots to the use of the famous deceased mathematician's alias to Charlie. The photo ID for Alan Turing was a match for Charlie."

"Wainwright was working with the Charlie and the Sureños? Why? It doesn't make any sense." Reeves couldn't accept what Izzy had discovered. There had to be a mistake…except Izzy didn't make mistakes.

"From the pattern between Wainwright and Charlie's calls, Charlie was the go-between with the Sureños until his death. Then Wainwright contacted the Sureños directly."

Reeves jerked back as if Finn did deliver the sucker punch. "It can't be true."

It meant that his mentor had ordered his kidnapping, had overdosed him with cocaine. Wainwright was the boss that McDonald and Muscle referred to. The entire time he was in the cell, Reeves imagined "the boss" as either a cartel don or a mob boss. And it was the man with whom he spent hours as a young man. A mentor Reeves had admired for his interest in his students and brilliant mind. A brilliant mind that had been used to manipulate a vulnerable man and kill an innocent soul.

"He has quite a nest egg that doesn't match a professor's salary. It's all hidden, but Molly and I were able to find it. He's recently received large payments, for which we're still working to trace the source, but the timing of the transfers fit with the attacks on the embassies. And the way the money has been moved globally smacks of the Russian connection we've been looking for.

"We're not sure how the Sureños became involved with the Russians, but Charlie must have been behind the hacking of the embassies. The timing of Tex's death after Charlie's accidental death works with the gaps. Wainwright needed the codes for the game after Charlie's death. Can you imagine his panic when he can't provide it to the Russians? And with the help of the very accommodating Sureños, he planned to extract it from Tex."

Darcy crossed the room and rested her hand on his arm. "I'm sorry, Reeves. I know what a shock it has to be."

Reeves stepped away. He couldn't pull it together. Not this second as he tried to grasp the evilness of a man he trusted.

"It adds up." Reeves slammed down any painful reactions to the betrayal of the people he respected. He switched to his logical, deductive side. Lucky for him, he had an incredible facility to compartmentalize.

"Charlie would have listened to Wainwright. He used Charlie, who was vulnerable and easy to exploit, to sell Charlie's skills to the Sureños, who went on to make a deal with the Russians." He spoke dispassionately. Dissecting a problem required ignoring that it involved people he cared about, people he entrusted with his heart. It was simple to deduce how Wainwright could manipulate Charlie with the promise of more wealth and stature.

"But Charlie had made a great deal of money from the game, right?" Danni asked.

"Charlie would always need more money to bolster his self-esteem. You know, we've seen it over and over again. Criminals that can never have enough money and power. And having a drug habit to feed, he probably ran through the cash quickly," Reeves said.

"If Wainwright was your mentor, why didn't he have access to the game? Or why didn't he write his own?" Sophie's blonde curls bounced as she shook her head.

"I'm with Sophie," Danni said. "What's Wainwright's motive? He could have developed his own game to sell to the Russians or do other lucrative schemes without involving Charlie."

"Wainwright wasn't involved in the development of the game. The three of us did all the work, and knowing it was a real breakthrough, we agreed never to share the game. Besides, Wainwright is brilliant theoretically but not in applied solutions.

He was never interested in spending hours creating code. He liked developing theoretical models. And manipulating Charlie would be a quick way to make a lot of money. Charlie would have trusted him."

"Let's go get the bastard. Now. I wanted revenge on the fucker for hurting you and Darcy." Danni lasered on Reeves. "But now knowing that he was someone you trusted…" Her voice was filled with outrage.

Reeves slung his arm over Danni's shoulder and dragged her close. "Thank you. I appreciate your willingness to help. But I need to settle this myself."

"That's enough touching." Lars grabbed Danni away.

"Don't kill the guy…yet," Izzy interjected. "We're following the money, but we have no way to connect him to the sale of ransomware, and the phones are circumstantial. We need access to his computer. Then, I'm sure, Reeves or I can extract the evidence from his computer to convict him of treason for selling American secrets."

"We're on it, Izzy," Nick said.

"Thanks, Izzy, especially since this isn't your case," Darcy added.

"Reeves is family. We geeks have to stick together to fight the evil powers. Danni and Sophie, you make sure he's getting loads of love…until I get back to Seattle."

Izzy clicked off before he could thank her. He replaced his phone in his pocket.

Everyone was waiting for him to say something. "Tomorrow, I'm going to visit Wainwright to see how he's feeling after having been poisoned." The pathetic thing was Reeves had already planned to check on him before he left Palo Alto.

"Don't drink any of the fucking scotch." Lars grinned.

Danni poked him in the ribs. "That's not funny. Reeves could have died."

"If he had died, I wouldn't have made the joke."

Finn and Nick, of course, cracked up.

Reeves would never be able to thank Lars for diverting

everyone's sympathetic looks. Wainwright had poured Reeves a large glass of the scotch, knowing it was laced with enough drug mixture to make him seize and possibly kill him as he had done to Tex.

"I'm going with you." Darcy searched his face, trying to read his reactions.

"I wouldn't expect anything less from an outstanding CIA agent. You came to Seattle to find the perpetrators of the ransomware. It will seal the deal for Libya if you can bag Wainwright."

"That isn't the reason I want to get Wainwright, and you know it."

He decided that the way her lips were pressed together wasn't endearing but a sign of her mulish personality.

"I'll need a distraction to get Wainwright out of his office to give me time to hack into his computer."

"Are you sure you can pull this off? The guy killed your friend and tried to kill you. No one would think less of you if you decided not to go." Darcy touched his arm again. "We can find other ways to access his office."

"Thanks for your concern. I'm not a master at dissimulation as you are, but I think I can handle myself."

"A fire alarm isn't enough. This guy is smart. We need something less pedantic," Finn said.

"The students are always protesting the IT department and its involvement in assisting the defense department in 'drones of death' and the use of AI to spy on citizens. We can use a fictional student group and stage a bomb threat to clear the building."

"With Richard on the Board of Directors, I don't think it will take a lot to set up. When he discovers Wainwright is behind your kidnapping, we'll have to rein Richard in. He'll want to blow up the entire building," Nick said.

"I'm surprised you've been able to stop Richard from showing up in Palo Alto," Reeves said.

"Jordan has kept him in Seattle. We all owe her."

"But Wainwright will expect Reeves and me to exit the building with him," Darcy said.

He could feel Darcy's stare but refused to look at her. Reeves would make sure Wainwright paid for what he had done to Tex and Charlie, and then he was finished. He'd head back to Seattle and put the whole experience in his rearview.

"Lars and I will make sure you're separated with no suspicions on Wainwright's part," Finn said.

"You have to play the harried visitor this time. I'll go in as the security guard," Lars added.

Finn rolled his eyes. "Whatever."

Reeves faked a yawn. "Looks as if you've got it handled. I'm crashing. It's been a long twenty-four hours."

"We've got your back." Nick paused, giving Reeves an inscrutable look. "Always."

The Jenkinses were all trained observers. He didn't fool anyone that he wasn't hurting.

Lars fist-bumped Reeves. And of course, Sophie had to hug him, which he prolonged to get the expected reaction from Finn and to distract everyone from focusing on him. The Jenkins were very possessive of their women. He understood. If he ever had a woman like Sophie or Danni…

He glanced at Darcy. She met his gaze with a defiant look.

"Let her go, Reeves. Now."

Sophie went on her tiptoes and kissed Reeves on the cheek. "Finn isn't serious because if he was…" Laughing, Sophie grabbed Finn's hand. "He'd be in big trouble."

Danni, six feet tall and very fit, was next to offer support. She squeezed Reeves hard. "You've always been there for all of us. We're here for you."

"Honey, lighten up the hold. The guy's had a rough night/day," Lars quipped.

Danni whispered, "Don't give up on her. She needs time. Look how long it took me to admit my feelings for Lars."

Reeves didn't want to wait. He knew how he felt, and less than eight hours ago, he thought he knew how Darcy felt.

"Thanks, everyone. See you in the morning." And without a glance at Darcy, he headed to his bedroom. The bedroom he thought he'd be sharing with Darcy.

CHAPTER NINETEEN

The silence in the room was unnerving after a subdued Reeves left.

Darcy would rather negotiate a release with the Taliban than face Reeves's very protective friends. She didn't shy away from confrontation. When duty called, she ran into the fire, but this was different.

These welcoming people weren't hostiles.

"You don't owe an explanation to any of us."

Danni had worn down all of Darcy's mistrust with her direct and caring manner. "Just don't jerk him around. Not right now. He's our friend, and he's hurting."

She hadn't thought her comment about Libya would upset him. She had been in shock that Director Marwick, happy with Richard Dean's praise, had offered a position that she didn't see getting until finishing at least five more years of hellhole assignments. She had been shocked by the way the balance had shifted and the power Richard Dean wielded. She wasn't sure how she felt about the whole thing, and she'd blurted it out.

"I'm glad that Reeves has such an incredible group of friends, especially right now when he's had so much thrown at him. And I have no intention of causing him any more distress. He and I need some time to sort things out."

"Is that what the kids are calling it now?" Lars winked at her.

Darcy hated that her skin was the color of a stop sign,

especially in front of the macho Marine Jenkinses. They had accepted her as a part of their team, acknowledging her training, but she wasn't used to sharing her feelings en masse, especially regarding her relationships.

Sophie didn't hesitate to pull Darcy into a hug. "You're good for him. But you have to decide if he's good for you. And we won't hold it against you if it doesn't work out."

"Of course, we'll think you're an idiot." Danni lifted one eyebrow.

During the time Danni and Sophie were helping her change, they had shared multiple stories illustrating what a good friend and a great brother Reeves had proven himself to be. They were shameless in their promotion of their friend. They had stopped before giving him an endorsement with animals and children.

The women also had confided how much they disliked Lily, Reeves's self-absorbed, demanding ex.

"She and Reeves don't need your meddling," Nick's deep voice boomed.

"I'm reporting to Emily your use of meddling in the context of my emotional support." Danni poked Nick in the chest. "You're already in the doghouse for not telling her about his kidnapping."

"Wait to report my newest blunder until Wainwright is in cuffs, Danni. Emily doesn't need to know about tomorrow. Not when she's on tour."

"I'm not planning on telling her. Believe it or not, my 'meddling' is helpful."

Nick nodded. "We've got a big day tomorrow. Everyone, get some rest."

"Come on, Danni. We have a lot to 'sort out' tonight." Lars wagged his eyebrows.

"You're right. We do have to finish the guest list and decide on the caterer."

Danni grinned at Lars's dramatic moan in response to the mention of wedding details.

Darcy had hoped that they would leave before she did. She didn't want them to see her go to Reeves's room. Her room too. He'd learn that soon enough.

"Good night. And thank you for including me as part of your team." Darcy looked at Nick and then the rest of the group. "I'm looking forward to nailing Wainwright tomorrow."

She walked toward Reeves's door, feeling every eye on her back. She entered without knocking.

As she stepped into the room, Reeves walked out of the bathroom wearing nothing but a towel wrapped around his hips, drying his hair with another one. And even though the large room was only lit by the bedside lamps, she saw the water glistening on his chiseled pecs, abs, and down his muscular thighs. The towel was too small to hide the inviting line of dark hair leading to an impressive bulge. For a tech geek, Reeves was a perfect specimen of maleness. And all hers to touch and kiss once they got their business settled.

"Did we get our room assignments wrong? This is my room." His tone was arctic and condescending.

She had to remind herself that he was in pain and not just being a jerk.

"My room as well." Taking a page out of Danni's playbook, Darcy moved closer and placed one hand on her hip.

"Your room?" He didn't stop rubbing his hair, displaying his sculpted biceps and the black hair under his arms.

Heat flooded through her. And her knees got shaky. His brooding, raw masculinity undid her.

She lowered her voice. "I never go back on my promises."

His hand stopped mid-air as his eyes narrowed on her. "I don't recall any promise."

He was going to make her pay, the big clod.

"You're such a liar. You know exactly what I'm talking about. I made a promise after your kidnapping to spend the night in bed with you if you listened to your body and rested."

"Forget it." He tossed the towel he dried his hair with onto the floor. "I don't need a pity fuck."

She marched right in front of him, close enough to breathe in the clean scent of soap combined with the musky scent of male.

"But if you're set on sleeping in this bed, go for it. I'll go upstairs."

Darcy, not known for patience with her idiot brothers, poked him hard in the chest. "Stop being such a big jerk. A 'pity fuck?' Really? If I had two available hands, I'd knock you on your ass."

He grabbed her finger. "Is that so?"

His breathing was audible, and the color on his cheeks darkened. She could bend and lick the water drips on the thick mat of hair on his chest—follow it down the path that winded to the real pleasure.

The sexual tension intensified with every uptick in his breath. She was primed, and the scent of arousal filled the air as her breasts swelled and her breathing quickened. She could barely control herself to not tear off his towel and get down on her knees.

He released her finger and stepped back, taking away the heat radiating off his body and his scent that fired her pheromones.

"Why are you here, Darcy?"

"You know why I'm here, Reeves. I want you. And the way the towel is tented, you want me too."

He moved to his suitcase lying on the floor, then bent over to allow a panoramic view of his male parts. And it was enough for her heart to skip a beat or two or even three.

"Means nothing except I'm a healthy male who responds to any woman showing up in my bedroom. But I'm not in the mood to take care of you tonight. I have an important day ahead of me tomorrow."

"Okay, jackass, that's it. I've had enough of you, 'Mr. Pissed Off, Poor Reeves.' Are you ready to marry me?"

He snapped around. "What the hell?"

She followed him, invading his space. "You heard the question. Are you ready to marry me?"

"Your concussion is affecting your thinking."

She loved the way his chest flexed and the towel loosened with his tirade. A girl could hope for a show.

"Then why are you angry and hurt that I'm not ready to marry you either?"

"Honestly, Darcy. I'm getting dressed to take you to a clinic for a CT scan. You're making no sense."

"I'm making total sense. You're acting as if I kick puppies and waterboard innocents because I might be awarded a dream job in the future. The *future*. A future we haven't had time to discuss. Hell, we barely know each other. Two days ago, we hadn't met in person. We haven't even had sex, but you're mad and rejecting me tonight because of a possibility that may never happen."

He ran his hand through his tousled hair, giving her another spectacular view of his armpit. Who knew she could get wet from any part of a well-formed man's anatomy? Not just any man. Reeves. Only Reeves. Every inch of Reeves was a turn-on.

"You're right. And I am mad. Mad at myself. I don't have your experience of living under the wire. I thought how I felt about you after my kidnapping was real and not an after-effect of all the emotions and adrenaline dump. But I've had time to think it through. And it was nothing but blind lust that got all mixed up after the threat. Nothing more."

Darcy controlled the need to roll her eyes and prayed for patience. Reeves had had shock piled upon shock since she'd arrived in his life.

"I do have more experience, but I've never thrown myself at any other man who has been part of an operation. I've never declared myself, never shared how terrified I was that I might have lost him. Never wanted a man as much as I want you, Reeves Hewitt."

"If you're looking for a no-strings fling before you leave for Libya, I'm not interested."

"Are you trying to test me, or are you that dense? I haven't decided anything about Libya. We just met. It isn't the time to make life decisions. Take the reverse. What if I told you, 'I'm leaving the CIA, taking the Jenkins job, and moving to Seattle.' You wouldn't think it's a little premature?"

"If you meant it, I'm ready for all of it. You had me when you walked into Richard's office, and I realized the sexy redhead was the incredible gamer XChoco. It's what I want. You and me together. I don't want you to give up your work to be a couple. But I do want you to leave the CIA because of the way they treat you. You deserve better. At Jenkins, you'd be respected. And Richard has global business all around the world where you could make a difference."

"And we would work together?" Darcy searched his face, looking for the gleam of teasing that he was joking.

"We wouldn't exactly be working together. I spend a great deal of my time at the software company. It's only when the situation gets harried, and the Jenkinses need my cyber skills, that I get involved. Nick and the men do their own thing."

"I'm a policeman's daughter. No ties to high society. And no interest in being groomed to fit into that lifestyle."

"So, you didn't like Sophie? You wouldn't want to have dinner with her and Finn?"

"No, Sophie is great and nothing like what I expected."

"Then that's easy since Soph and Jordan are family. And you can't go higher than them in Seattle society. So that's not a problem." He lifted her chin with a finger. "What's this really about it, honey?"

She looked into his eyes. She was trained to trust her gut, and her gut was shouting that Reeves was the most wonderful man and she'd be making a mistake by not pursuing their connection. But she had never made a leap of faith like this before.

"Are you always this impulsive? How can you be so sure about us?"

He shrugged, and the towel slipped lower, riding on his hips.

She tried to keep her eyes focused on his face. This was a serious conversation.

"I just know. And for a mathematical nerd, it's insane and illogical not to have facts and trust some unknown quantity. But I do know. Can I show you how I know?"

There was the teasing glint that she loved in his eyes.

He lifted her in his arms against his naked, hot chest. "It might take me all night to prove my theory."

"I'm going to be hard to convince." She rubbed against his erection.

"As you can feel, I have hard evidence to support my point of view."

CHAPTER TWENTY

Reeves carried Darcy to the bed. His body was one rigid muscle. The scent of her arousal and her lemon shampoo filling his nostrils was a powerful aphrodisiac—as if he needed any inducement to want Darcy. He wanted her since the moment he spotted her in Richard's office—all buttoned-up, at attention, her lips pressed together in distaste at being forced to work with him. Her passionate nature was as her flaming red hair that couldn't be kept tightly secure, always slipping out of its confines.

He would like to drop her on the bed and crawl right on top of her, but Darcy deserved gentleness and tenderness. Damn, the woman was still restrained in a splint, and her face was a rainbow of purple-and-yellow bruising.

He wanted to make this perfect for her, but the way she was nibbling on his earlobe and sucking on his neck was tearing apart the last threads of his tightly held control.

"I love this stubble and the strong jawline and the classic Grecian nose." She ran her finger along his nose before returning down to his lips, which she traced with her fingertip.

"This is my favorite—your lips." She giggled. "Well, not my favorite." She lifted and pressed down against his erection. "Favorite that I'm familiar with. I'm not acquainted with this part of you yet. But I plan to become intimately friendly with all of you."

He moaned when she repeated the movement. The idea of

Darcy and his dick having an intimate relationship made him expand and pulsate. He defied science, swelling bigger, growing harder.

"I'm not sure if it's your lips or your eyes that are my second favorite. I like it when you get the smallest quirky smile, and your lip turns up at this corner."

Her mouth came close to his, hovered, and waited.

The nearness of her was like explosive kindling, igniting sparks of fire down his spine to his balls.

His hand slid under her thick hair, curled around her neck, pulling her near. Finally, her lips brushed his, the mere touch inflaming him to a flashpoint. He tilted her chin and licked her lips, teasing her mouth open.

Her mouth clung to his. Loving the feel of her warm, full lips against his, he kissed her as he had been dreaming about, exploring her plump, pillowy heat. She tasted so good, like a sugary dessert, causing an intense craving for more. He was already addicted to kisses by Darcy Wilson.

He lowered her down the length of him in a long, sexy slide. Reveling in the sensation of every inch of contact with her. His dick throbbed with tantalizing anticipation.

She hung onto him, her body melting against him. With her against him, he deepened the kiss, pushing his tongue past her teeth to slide along the length of hers.

His tongue teased before she kissed him with desperate hunger, her mouth devouring him. He answered with the same desperation. He lost track of time with Darcy kissing him with singular focus as if he were her mission.

He grabbed her sweet ass and tipped her against him, never breaking contact with her lips.

She tugged on his lower lip, sucking it between her teeth. "I could spend the entire night exploring, kissing, licking in all my favorite places."

Her words made all his blood rush south, and his body stiffened into full readiness.

He trailed kisses down the delicate curve of her neck, pausing at the little notch at the base of her throat where her pulse thrummed. He placed his lips against her pulse, sucking lightly.

Darcy's head dropped back, exposing the long, glorious line of her neck. He traced her pulsing vein first with his finger and then with his tongue. Primitive feelings rushed through him. He wanted to mark her as his own, suck on her pale skin. But going to work in her standard white blouse, Darcy wouldn't appreciate his male possessiveness.

He fingered the tiny straps on the black dress, continuing his exploration of her delicate collarbone and shoulder. "This dress was Danni's idea, wasn't it? She and Sophie were enjoying watching me squirm, fighting a boner. God, it took all my control to keep it down. Thank God for jeans."

She looked up at him, her eyes drowsy with desire. "It was the only dress that would easily fit over my splint. Nothing about driving you crazy."

He raised her silky hair and nuzzled behind her ear. "Liar. You knew exactly the effect you were having on me."

She giggled. Miss "Seriously, the world might end" giggled. "Maybe a little."

"You must have been an adorable little girl. All curls and freckles." The image of a giggling little Darcy flashed in his mind. And surprising himself, Reeves welcomed the possibility of loving a girl with a mop of curls, and freckles, and sparkly green eyes like Darcy.

"Can we talk about my childhood later? I want to see you naked." Her skin was dewy and flushed a pretty pink.

"I can do something about that." With one quick move, he dropped the towel on the floor.

Darcy covered her mouth to hide her laughter. "I didn't mean it literally, like right this second."

"Honey, you tell a man you want to see him naked, this is what you get." His muscles were pumping from intense blood flow, and his erection was at full mast. He put his hands on his hips. "You better not be laughing at my junk, or we're going to have a problem."

Darcy threw herself at him, grabbing him and holding tight

with her one arm. "Reeves, you're a beautiful man, but…you're the only man who can make me laugh in the middle of blinding, needy lust."

"I'm not sure making you laugh is a compliment." Her heat against his skin abraded every nerve cell, as did her hot words. He couldn't stop his hips from flexing against her.

"Can you help me out of this dress?" Darcy stepped away, taking all her heat and softness.

"It's probably best to keep your splint on. We'll have to work around it." He lowered the strap. "Is it better if you step out of your dress? That way, you don't have to lift your arms?"

He slowly slid the strap off and then pressed kisses on her shoulder. "You have the softest skin with these little bursts of fire. It will take a lifetime to pay full homage to your freckles."

He carefully lowered the strap more over her splinted arm, and the dress fell to the floor, exposing her full, pale breasts, her erect nipples, and the tiny scrap of a pink lace thong. He couldn't move, mesmerized, enthralled, and pulsing with need.

"Darcy, you take away my breath. I'm…lost for words. I'm never lost for words!"

She backed onto the bed, kicking off her flip-flops, and fell against the pillows. Her red hair spread across the pillow as he had fantasized. "So, you're not thinking of Python or Java right now?"

Her eyes sparkled in delight. He always wanted his stern, by the book woman as playful and happy as she was in this minute.

"Darlin', I'm thinking what a lucky bastard I am to have you in my bed. Ms. Darcy Wilson, the CIA's most lethal weapon. I've been waiting for you my entire life."

"Reeves, I feel the same. I never knew a man like you could exist." She opened her one arm in invitation. "Make love to me. I want you, only you."

His heart thrashed against his chest. This was the sweetest torture imaginable to have Darcy all laid out for him. He hesitated. If he got on top of her, it would be over too soon. He wanted more for their first time. It had to be everything she deserved—to be cherished, loved for the incredible woman she was.

"What's wrong, Reeves?"

"I can't decide where to begin." He stretched out on the bed beside her, his hand traveling up one of her calves, to her thigh, to the curve of her hip. As he gently brushed her skin, his senses were on overload by her beauty.

"Let me help you." Guiding his fingers, she pressed them against the tiny panties covering her wet mound. "I'm partial to you starting here."

He chuckled, but his brain jammed as his dick twitched with her on wonderous display next to him, her thatch of red hair visible through the nearly see-through panties. Her red hair was such a turn-on. His dick, rock hard, was ready to explode.

"Oh, but I wanted to start here."

Her skin was smooth as satin. His fingertips tingled as he stroked down her chest to her breasts. His palm burned when he cupped the soft weight. Each breast filled his hand.

Darcy dragged in a slow and shuddering breath but didn't protest. She watched, desire glowing in her eyes, as he lifted and stroked her, taking his time to knead and plump the firm mounds. He rolled each nipple between his fingers into tight buds.

Darcy threw her head against the pillow with her eyes closed. Her skin was flushed. Her lips parted. This was how he wanted her, lost in sensation.

He pulled the warm flesh into his mouth. Pleasure streaked through him. Suckling her was another addiction he might have for life. A primitive neanderthal, he wanted to be the only man ever to see her, touch her, taste her honeyed nipples.

Darcy whimpered and opened her legs. He switched to her other breast, sucking hard.

He skimmed his hand down, caressing the rounded curve of her hip. He traced the soft lines of her body, tangling his fingers underneath her panties into the red curls.

Darcy arched off the bed, drawing out his name in a pleading tone. "Reeeeves."

His heart pounded against his chest and his dick throbbed from her entreaty. Darcy's pleading would be added to his growing list.

He groaned as a sharp and painful burn lanced through him when he discovered her bud already hard, throbbing, and welcoming.

"Is this what you needed, baby?" And he pulled, his teeth scraping her nipple as he pressed one finger into her wet sheath and slid farther, probing between her slick folds, then pushing deep. And deeper, igniting fire. She screamed his name as she spasmed around his fingers, the sweet fever taking her.

Her shudders were almost his undoing. He had to focus on watching Darcy and not the need to sink into her, to fill her empty space made for him, feel her spasms surrounding him.

"Reeves, I need you now. I have an ache only you can fill."

Triumph soared through him.

She reached to stroke his erection. Her touch left him shaking, gasping, struggling to gain any glimmer of control.

"But I wanted…"

Darcy squeezed him hard. "What about what I want?"

Reeves couldn't argue with that. He could barely get words out. Anticipation skittered across his skin.

"Will it be easier if you ride me?" As he uttered the words, raw lust swamped his body.

Her eyes gleamed, catching the light from the bedside lamp. "I'd like that. The powerful stud, Reeves Hewitt, beneath me. Maybe later…"

He reached into the drawer for a condom to suit up.

"I thought you might." He laughed. She wasn't like other women. She was bold and aggressive, intent on shredding all of his control, all of his defenses. And he loved it.

"I think I'll be very comfortable just like this." She spread her legs and ran her hand over her breast.

Excitement whirled as he melded his lips against her, their tongues dancing as he lowered himself on top of her. Heat and warm, pliant flesh surrounded him as the need between them rose to a crescendo.

His kisses became demanding, commanding. She belonged to him. Only him. He would never let her go. Did she understand what this meant?

Reeves climbed her body as if he were a conquering hero and settled between her legs. "I can't take it slow as I hoped."

"Later. Right now, I want it hard and fast. Make me feel every impressive inch of you, Reeves."

He sent a silent hallelujah to the gods who brought Darcy into his life as he slid into her.

And once he was fully impaled in her snug, moist heat, he waited. He didn't want to hurt her. He was a big man, and she was a tiny woman. When he looked down, their eyes met in silent communion, their breaths and bodies mingling as one.

He waited for her to adjust, sweat pouring down his back and beading on his forehead, not willing to move until she was ready.

Her nails scored his back as she lifted her hips to bring them closer. And he started to move, increasing his speed until he pounded into her.

She drew her knees up, planting her heels into the mattress, pushing up to meet him thrust for thrust.

Adjusting his position to put pressure on her clitoris, he kept up the pace in that position. She squeezed her eyes shut; her pants whispered across his face as he quickened. She flung her head back and cried out.

Her spasms squeezed him tight. He marveled at his control. He paused to watch Darcy ride the wave of pleasure, her skin glistening, the smell of sex giving off a heady scent. She was beautiful in her passion.

He stared at her as he plunged. Communicating with his body his need to be united with her in the most primitive way. She belonged to him as he belonged to her with each thrust.

She pulled him down to kiss him tenderly. A soft brush of her lips before her hand cupped his face. "Reeves."

Her eyes were wide open with love, and his name was enough. He didn't need any other words as he drove into her one last time and spilled his seed.

"I know, honey. Me too." He pressed to his forearms to take his weight off of her, but he didn't want to pull out of her body. Not yet. Not after how long he had waited.

"But…" She started.

He pressed his finger to her lips, swollen from his kisses. "Not here in our bed. Here we only share our connection. Can you trust me that we will work everything out?"

"I trusted you the minute I met you and hated you for it. I wanted you to be the bad guy."

"Sorry to disappoint you."

"You didn't disappoint me tonight." She raised her eyebrows, mimicking his movement.

He nudged himself against her. "Never, Darcy Wilson. I promise to do my best to always make you happy."

CHAPTER TWENTY-ONE

Reeves and Darcy walked side by side toward the entrance of the IT building. Strands of her red hair caught the sunlight, intertwining gold with filaments of fire like the explosive woman she was in bed. There was truth to redheads being passionate women. She was demanding and responsive—pushing him to new heights of honesty and emotional connection. A blending together of not knowing where one stopped and the other began. Having Darcy next to him, a partner in bed, a partner in this undertaking, and a partner to walk with into the future would make his world complete…after today.

He was relatively calm despite his heart pounding against his chest, echoing like a Grave Digger concert. Darcy had instantly transformed since they exited the car, from a relaxed and sated Darcy into a high-alert, full battle soldier.

He took in a deep breath and slowly released it to center himself. The Jenkinses had spent the early morning running through the setup with him and Darcy. The men had been relentless, demanding constant repetition of every movement of the plan to commit the actions to muscle memory. Nothing was overlooked. And every variation was planned for possible complications. Their approach was perfected by ex-spec ops forces, so Reeves followed their lead. *Learn from the experts. Develop your techniques from their experiences.*

Finn had worked with Reeves on how not to inadvertently signal Wainwright with either body language or facial tells. Reeves had woken a few times during the night worrying that he might not be able to mask his horror and anger once he saw Wainwright.

The timing was a little tricky since Lars and Finn would make sure they were separated from Wainwright. Darcy and Reeves had to run down the stairs and be outside soon after Wainwright and after downloading his computer.

Darcy squeezed his arm when he released another deep breath.

"You've got this. Remember, don't lead with your emotions."

He would have laughed if the situation weren't dead serious. He had led with his emotions, enabling him to capture the woman of his dreams. But it wasn't the right technique to capture a sociopath. And Wainwright was a sociopath.

Reeves was ready to finish this and get on with his life with Darcy. To avenge his friends, knowing that he had destroyed Wainwright as the man had done to Tex and Charlie. Maybe it made Reeves a lesser man for not considering forgiveness. Maybe it would come with time. When his and Darcy's house was filled with grandchildren.

They neared the bank of elevators in the sleek new building. The computer science unit generated all the income for the entire mathematical department. Many of the graduates donated to their alma mater after they made their millions with their tech companies. The building looked more like it belonged in the center of Silicon Valley and not on a university campus.

Reeves stepped back to allow her to enter the elevator. He had to remember to always stay on Darcy's left to not impede her firing hand.

Darcy slowed and inspected the elevator. He wasn't sure what she expected to find.

Darcy's body tightened further if that were possible. Her spine was ramrod stiff, her eyes scanning every inch of the space. Her hesitant and vigilant entrance raised the little hairs on his neck. Knowing there were likely cameras in the elevator and not underestimating Wainwright's ability to hack them, he pulled

Darcy close as if in an affectionate nuzzle. "What's wrong?"

"The panel in the ceiling isn't completely closed. It could be purely accidental, but I don't like it. We'll take the stairs."

Trusting Darcy's instincts, he followed her out. "You do know that his office is on the twelfth floor."

"Yep, so time to show off your cardio fitness." Darcy moved fast toward the stairwell door.

"You want to race?"

"Smart-ass. Let's go. We don't want to throw off the time frame, so we're going to have to book it."

It was too late to change the timing. Nick would initiate the bomb threat twenty minutes after their arrival at Wainwright's office. Enough time hopefully not to link the threat to their visit and not too long of a time for Reeves to lose it from being in Wainwright's company.

Darcy wasn't joking that they had to book it. He didn't say anything about the risk of entering a stairwell. Darcy would have weighed the options and the risk.

Darcy led, which gave him plenty of time to watch her hips and ass work in the pants that somehow Danni and Sophie produced, along with shoes she could run in. She was extremely fit, but Reeves wasn't getting the work out that she was with her short legs.

When they reached the seventh floor, she stopped, bent over, and took deep breaths before checking her watch. "Sixteen minutes. We're cutting it short. We'll have to pick up the pace."

He didn't comment.

"Okay, I have to pick up my pace. I can't help that I'm height challenged."

"There is nothing wrong with you. You're perfect."

She huffed before she raced up the stairs. Looking over her shoulder, she said, "And don't be staring at my ass. Focus on the mission."

"Yes, ma'am." He grinned.

Without warning, a loud explosion detonated. It was hard to pinpoint where the blast had taken place in the walled cement stairwell, but it was in the building and close. It had to be powerful since the metal handrails vibrated through the concrete.

Without a pause, Darcy took off up the stairs.

Reeves's initial response was to go down to ground level, but he followed Darcy.

She shouted, her breathing unaffected by the grueling pace she set, "Wainwright knew we're coming. We need to stop him before he hurts anyone else."

Reeves's brain was catching up to the last seconds and how the game had changed dramatically. "That was the elevator?"

He took the steps two at a time to keep up. Who knew she could move that fast, even wearing a splint? The woman was amazing.

"Yep."

The realization of what Wainwright had planned for him and Darcy fueled Reeves. If she hadn't been vigilant, the bastard would have killed Darcy, the light of his world, without any remorse. Reeves intended to strangle the last breath out of the fucker. It wasn't enough that Wainwright killed his friends. Now he would have killed Darcy.

Darcy didn't miss a beat. "Sureños must have a mole in the police department who alerted Wainwright to the bomb threat."

Nick had to warn the Palo Alto police to their practice drill on campus so the entire county's police and fire departments wouldn't respond to a false alarm. The team had discussed the possibility of Wainwright being tipped off and decided not to alert the chief until an hour before the drill. Despite their careful planning, not even the spec ops had foreseen Wainwright blowing up an elevator.

Darcy waited at the door to the twelfth floor. She raised her hand to pause before pulling out her new Sig.

Right behind her, he reached for his Glock. They had both worn jackets to conceal their weapons, which made for a hot run up the stairs.

Sweat glistened on her forehead from the sprint in a suit jacket. Her focus and intensity were centered on him. Her eyes searched his, her pretty wheels spinning options of how to accomplish their mission and keep him safe.

"Don't consider it. I'm not staying in the stairwell."

"Fine. But you stick to me like white on rice. And nothing heroic to defend me."

"Got it. Be adhesive and do nothing stupid." He was willing to abide by her lead. He wasn't an idiot, but she was his woman, and he would protect her. Best not to put words to the thought right now.

She rolled her eyes. "He's desperate and unpredictable. Our goal is to take him in. Not kill him."

She was good. She had read his intention not to follow the team's plans but do a little revenge-hunting.

"Roger that."

"Make sure you do, or this could go sideways."

She slowly opened the door, peering both ways, and entered the empty hallway. Reeves was next. His thumping heart was the only sound he could hear in the eerie silence.

Darcy crept along the hallway toward Wainwright's office. She never stopped scanning the walls, ceilings, the floors, or looking for booby traps. Paranoid was good, really good at this moment.

The burst of adrenaline had pumped his muscles and laser-focused his brain. He was rearranging the game pieces, trying to anticipate Wainwright's next moves. Reeves had thought he'd have the satisfaction of outwitting him, but Wainwright was always two steps ahead of them because of his inside knowledge. It ended today.

Wainwright couldn't have anticipated that they hadn't taken the elevator, so their visit would be unexpected. If he hadn't already taken his computer and made a run for it. Reeves wouldn't allow the possibility that Wainwright had escaped.

No more from this maniac. Reeves planned to see to it personally.

He kept watch on their backs, wanting to ensure no surprises from the rear.

In front of Wainwright's office door, Darcy raised her gun hand for him to halt. Would they storm the office or wait for Nick and the team? He wanted to burst into the office and stop the maniac, but he didn't like the idea of Darcy directly in the line of the fire.

Darcy whispered. "You open the door. Then I'll go right, and you'll go left." Since Darcy was one-handed and right-handed, the plan was perfect. And at that moment, he had absolute clarity. He and Darcy were totally in sync, just as they had been in the *Snakes Ahead* game. They had worked as a team and had beat all odds against the bad guys. Today would be no different. He and Darcy were formidable and would vanquish the enemy. His breathing and his racing heart settled. He was in his battle zone, ready for anything and everything.

Reeves went left into the spacious area. Wainwright was bent over his PC open on its separate desk, close to the window, likely wiping it clean.

"Stop! Step away from the computer. Nice and slowly," Darcy commanded in a voice Reeves had never heard before.

The bastard smiled. "Reeves's girlfriend. It was a clever ploy to present a Fed as your girlfriend, but not clever enough."

Wainwright looked the same in a crumpled Oxford shirt, half-tucked into his wrinkled pants, a pair of glasses on the top of his head. His distinguished voice, with his clear dictation, was the same. Everything was the same. But everything had changed. This man had murdered his friends and was still trying to murder him and Darcy.

"Why?" Reeves was as shocked by his question as Darcy, who stopped in her move to get closer to Wainwright. "You have everything—full professor, chair of the department, international recognition."

Reeves had to understand. He had labeled Wainwright as evil and a sociopath to explain and distance himself. But now, standing in the familiar office with someone he had thought he had known and cared about, he had to understand…to solve the problem. To make sense of this twisted world that was now upside down and inside out. It was what he excelled at.

Wainwright took a step toward Reeves.

Darcy leveled her Sig at Wainwright. "Don't move."

"Darcy, you must be CIA or deep undercover in the FBI. None of my contacts could find anything on you, which made you an intriguing problem."

Reeves bristled at Wainwright's use of Darcy's name. One good thing—Darcy's cover wasn't blown.

"Darcy has nothing to do with this."

Wainwright shrugged. "You were the best of the three. I'm not surprised that you'd be the hardest to outwit. Poor Charlie with all of his childhood baggage, and poor Theodore, too shy and awkward to make a life for himself. But you—always a shining star and then the ultimate reward, working for Richard Dean, the billionaire who is royally treated when he deems to make an appearance on campus."

The bile rose in Reeves's gullet. He might be sick after listening to Wainwright's indifferent account of his dead friends and his jealousy of Richard.

"It was Richard who put the bug in my ear. You know that he often speaks here. Richard is quite a curious man with a breadth of interests. He was expounding on your success. How grateful he was to me for my tutelage. He was impressed that you made your first million before he had. And that was the moment I hatched my plan. Years of dedicating my life to students for what? Lucky to receive a bottle of scotch at Christmastime, to have the 'honor' of introducing Dean when he spoke on campus. It was a brilliant plan except that Charlie was an erratic partner. After he overdosed, I discovered in the last weeks that I excel at being a criminal. And it was easy until you and Darcy got involved."

Red, blistering rage exploded behind Reeves's eyes. "This was all for money? You killed Charlie and Tex for money? You sold out your country to the Russians for cash?"

"To be precise, I didn't kill either of them. Charlie killed himself, and Tex was killed by the Sureños. And you'll never connect me—you'll never connect me to anything. You might be smart, but I've always been smarter."

"But you don't deny you sold out your country."

Wainwright shrugged. "I wanted to watch Richard Dean, the billionaire who consults with presidents, be accused of being complicit in treason because of his connection with you. I must say the plan was magnificent to use 'your' game to make millions and bring about Richard Dean's downfall. How many DOD contracts do you think Dean would win after the accusation? It doesn't matter if they were false. He'd be tried and found guilty in the public eye."

Reeves had no response. Nothing. He was empty of emotion.

"Let's go, Wainwright. I'm sure we'll find something for you to spend time on behind bars." Darcy moved in.

Reeves didn't like that they had nothing to restrain Wainwright. He didn't trust him, and he sure as hell didn't like how close Darcy was to the villain.

And suddenly, it happened in a blur. Wainwright extracted a knife from his long sleeve in a surprisingly deft motion. Coming from the side, Darcy struck the knife out of his hand with one swift and forceful kick. Wainwright didn't stop but charged Reeves.

Reeves leveled his Glock. Darcy fired faster, hitting Wainwright in his lower leg.

Wainwright dropped to the ground, writhing as the blood flowed on the rug.

Darcy kept her gun on Wainwright. "I'll need you to check him for any other weapons. I'm a little hampered here."

"Not too hampered. Nice shooting, babe."

Darcy shook her head. "Are you all right?"

The door burst open. Finn and Lars exploded into the space with their guns raised. Looking at their aggressive and intimidating entrance, Reeves was glad they were on his side.

Finn dropped to the floor and searched Wainwright as the man moaned and demanded medical care and his lawyer.

"Took you long enough." Reeves's hands and knees were a little shaky as he put his gun back. Darcy was right. Shooting at the practice range was not the same as shooting a person. But Reeves knew he would have shot Wainwright to protect Darcy.

"We've been a little busy since we didn't know if you and Darcy were on the elevator." Lars lifted his eyebrows. "Nick was beside himself, thinking he'd have to explain it to Emily."

"Nick and I bet that Darcy wouldn't have gotten on the elevator. Lars wasn't as confident…you being Army and all," Finn added.

Darcy stepped over Wainwright, tucking her gun away, and walked to Reeves. He wrapped his arm around her shoulder and led her out of the office away from Wainwright, away from the pain that one pathetic person had caused. Reeves didn't fool himself that this drama was finished. It would take time, time with Darcy to heal himself and find a way to put this insanity in some kind of perspective.

He tightened his hold on her. "Just like in *Snakes Ahead*, you covered me. How lucky I am to have a superhero as my partner."

"And you stopped the bad guys from crossing the bridge to get to me. You know I'll always cover you, Reeves."

"As I will you, XChoco."

EPILOGUE

One month later

Darcy plopped back on the pillows, breathlessly in awe of her lover. "Unbelievable. How do you do it?"

Reeves, his chest glistening in sweat, on his knees astride her, loomed over her. "First, you have to be naked. And then, I take my…"

Darcy grabbed and twisted his chest hair. "Smart-ass. I'm not talking about mechanics."

He leaned forward and pushed the curls away from her face, his chest abrading her already sensitive nipples from their latest bout of lovemaking. After their night of riotous sex, she would need extra time to flat iron her hair to get it into a clip for her meeting today.

"How we feel about each other makes the difference." His lips quirked up in the corner, and his eyes lit with amusement and challenge.

He got off on teasing her. There were times when she didn't think his teasing was endearing. Like now.

"You're going to make me say it first, aren't you? Just so you can lord it over me?"

Neither of them had taken the next step in their relationship and said the three magic words. Reeves was waiting for her to go first. For a genius, he could be slow on the uptake. So, she wasn't great at sharing her feelings. She demonstrated how she felt by her actions. And taking a leave of absence from the CIA to consult with Jenkins Security should be proof enough of her feelings for the gorgeous man now skewering her with an intense stare.

"I'm keeping to our agreement that we would take our relationship nice and slow. No pressure. We're in the middle of a trial run, testing whether Jenkins Security and Seattle is the right career choice for you."

"You know, you can sometimes be an idiot." She wrapped her legs around his waist, grabbed his shoulders, tightened her hold, and flipped him on his back.

Reeves, anticipating her move, showed no resistance. He laughed. "You need to find other ways of expressing your frustration, honey."

On top of him, she rubbed against his growing erection. "You don't like my way?"

"I love your mating methods." He pressed against her, distracting her from the conversation. "You can do this. You're the woman who shot Wainwright. You're a tough ass. Star CIA officer."

Capturing Wainwright was a career changer for her. She now had options with the CIA and more control over her next assignment. She was a superstar at the agency at this moment. She knew from experience it wouldn't last.

The CIA director had given her a six-month leave of absence after exemplary work on the ransomware case. It was pretty unheard of, but Richard Dean's influence played a major part in the director's generosity. Richard, of course, denied it.

Wainwright gave up his Russian connections to the CIA for leniency. The information had moved up the food chain in the CIA. It was a big win for the agency.

She also was given credit for linking the Sureños with a foreign power. Charging the Sureños with treason gave the FBI leverage to build a case against the entire organization. Also, a win for interagency cooperation and a feather in the FBI's cap.

She hesitated. It was harder than she thought. "My career choice is probationary, but not us. I wouldn't uproot my life if I weren't committed."

His hot hands rubbed her back in soothing circles. "And if this international gig with Richard doesn't work, then we'll move to DC or Libya or wherever the CIA sends you. You're quite the negotiator…especially when you're naked."

Richard had offered her an incredible job. She would be a consultant for his international security. Working in tandem with Jenkins, she'd be in charge of establishing relationships with assets across the globe. She had it all. Global work to make a difference and belonging to a group of professionals she admired. In the CIA, you were on your own. She hadn't realized how isolated she had become until working with the Jenkinses—how much she missed her brothers and being part of a raucous family.

Reeves had agreed to leave his job if Darcy wasn't happy in Seattle. Compromise was never easy for her, but Reeves made it simple. He had enough confidence not to be threatened by her need for a challenging career and to exert control over her life. What she couldn't control were her feelings for Reeves. She never anticipated how loving someone would change everything you perceived as important. She had spent so much time proving herself, and with Reeves, she had no need. He loved her as she was.

She leaned over and tenderly brushed her lips across his. "I love you, Reeves Hewitt. No one else. Never will love anyone but you. I want adventures with you."

"Now that wasn't so hard, was it?" His eyes gleamed with humor.

"I love you, Darcy Wilson. And I plan to spend a lifetime providing you with adventures…starting right now."

And with one smooth move, he flipped her on her back.

Darcy laughed. There were times when losing was a win. Not that she would ever admit it under pain of death to Reeves.

Dear Reader,

Thank you for reading *Mission: Impossible to Deny*! I hope you enjoyed it. If you did, please help others find it by writing an online review at your favorite retailer or Goodreads!

Reviews mean so much to an independent author and I love reading them.

Please sign up for my newsletter to see the latest news, and join my readers group to the be first to hear about special events, excerpts, and unseen previews.

Visit my website to sign up and to read more about me and my books. Page ahead to find excerpts from two of my other books. Thank you!

— *Jacki*

www.jackidelecki.com

Enjoy an excerpt from

CHAPTER ONE

Hugging the backstage wall, Danni Knorr crept in the shadows with her SIG tucked into her skirt and a flashlight in her hand. The only light in the wings came from the red exit sign. The band's frenetic sound matched her heartbeat as it raced to its own crazy-ass rhythm. Espionage beat the hell out of spending the day in a biochemistry/physics lab. Undercover as rock star Alex Hardy's girlfriend/bodyguard, she had discovered a new high. Like drinking expensive French champagne, she got off on danger.

This was a new thing. Before she'd been kidnapped, Danni had never thought about her body more than keeping it in shape and healthy. Had never thought of holding a gun, let alone buying one and practicing with targets weekly. Had never realized just how many threats were out there and how little she'd been able to do to save herself.

Honing her body into a fighting machine with Krav Maga had been her first step to taking charge after she had been kidnapped. Then she'd taken classes on tactical awareness. She'd read up on the FBI and various police trainings. She'd even thought about joining the Jenkins Security agency, but Nick Jenkins had turned her down because of her lack of experience. At least he'd been honest with her.

The last step in her "recovery" was to take ownership of her pleasure. Sex with the famous superstud Alex Hardy was to be the ultimate statement of her proclaimed freedom. She hadn't yet made up her mind whether she should seduce him.

Right now, acting only as his bodyguard suited her perfectly. Her idea to guard the musician after discovering that he was being stalked had been serendipitous. A year ago, when Jax the Jerk, her ex-fiancé, had left her at the altar for a teenager with more enthusiasm and experience with sex than she had—or so he'd been happy to tell her—Danni had been unable to bite the bullet and seduce any guy. Since then, there was only one man who'd tempted her to open up and be vulnerable as well as passionate, and sadly, it wasn't Alex, no matter how much she tried to persuade herself to give him a chance.

Danni stopped and hid against the black concrete wall, searching for the location of the backstage crew before she went into the greenroom. She could easily bullshit about why she was wandering backstage, away from Alex's performance, but she'd rather not draw attention to herself. And she preferred to avoid creepy Frank, Alex's childhood friend and head of security.

The murmur of the crew's voices could be heard outside the stage door where they took their breaks to vape cancer. They had twenty minutes of downtime before the next scene change, allowing Danni less than fifteen minutes to search the belongings of the band and the traveling staff before the backstage crew would be back at work, and the band would take their break in the greenroom.

She knew she was grasping at straws trying to connect the band and staff to Alex's stalker. But Danni was determined to find how the stalker had accessed Alex's dressing room to leave the third threatening letter at the last concert in Portland.

Posing as Alex's girlfriend, she had flown to every city for the last four weeks to hang with the band and the groupies and have her picture taken with Alex. She had declined traveling in the almost all-male—except for Luna, the drummer's girlfriend and the band's massage therapist—tour bus, no matter how luxurious their RVs were.

Six cities and all their fake PDA, hoping to bait the stalker to reveal herself, and they had nothing except for another letter. Danni was no further along, with not one lead on how the stalker had breached Alex's dressing room in Portland.

She slowly opened the door to make sure that the greenroom was clear of the catering staff or aggressive groupies.

Despite the name, the room where the band members hung out during breaks and before the show wasn't green. As the headliner, Alex had his own dressing room. The greenroom in LA was no different from any of the other performers' backstage rooms she'd seen the past months.

She decided to snoop without Alex's knowledge. He was too close to his band and would never believe that one of them could be the stalker. And he most likely was right since there was a ridiculously low probability. But the band and traveling staff all had access to Alex's dressing room, and they were the only consistent factor since the backstage crews changed in every city. She needed to be absolutely sure that the stalker wasn't a disgruntled band or traveling staff member.

Guitar cases, gym bags, and backpacks were scattered across the worn industrial carpet. Being on tour wasn't as cool as everyone imagined. It was exhausting, with boring hours of tedious downtime for the two-to-three-hour high of performance. But, like her newly found danger addiction, performing was a high that fed on itself.

A half-open leather backpack was propped haphazardly against a guitar case. She knew exactly which mess belonged to which member, making it easy to start—Roland Young, drug addict, and the lead guitarist made the top on her list. She didn't have a clear connection between his addiction and stalking Alex, but he was the only member who raised red flags.

She hurried across the nondescript room, which was painted purple to create an edgy feel in the utilitarian square space. Kneeling next to the beat-up leather backpack, she began a methodical search. She didn't know what she might find, but she trusted her instincts to recognize a clue.

Her hands shook as the adrenaline surged through her body—part of the thrill of the hormonal rollercoaster. Maybe she had read too many Nancy Drew novels as a young girl.

She went through each pocket—a row of condoms, spiking hair gel, a bag of Reese's Peanut Butter Cups. Pretty dull findings. Despite being a junky with an oversized ego, nothing suspicious linked Roland to the stalker or even revealed obvious drug paraphernalia.

The center of the pack held deodorant, and two rolled-up T-shirts that he'd change into at the breaks in the set. She shook out both—nada.

She scooted over to Roland's guitar case and unlatched it. Besides being illegal, this was a ridiculous waste of time.

Danni stopped in response to a possible sound from the hallway. Her heart jolted at the fear of being discovered. She turned quickly to the crew's side door, where she had just entered. She strained to hear whether anyone was approaching. Part of the downside of the adrenaline rush was it made you hyperalert and a bit overreactive. A possible advantage when your life was in danger. Not great when you're just snooping and needed to remain undetected.

When no one appeared, she rifled through Roland's case. Nothing but extra sets of strings and picks. Although Roland was a slob, he took good care of his guitars.

She methodically went through everyone else's gear with no findings. Checking her phone, she realized she better hurry back to Alex's dressing room to make sure there were no surprises waiting for him during his break. She now checked Alex's room before he returned between sets.

Danni was hurrying back toward Alex's room when the dressing room door opened. She stepped to the side of a giant speaker to watch who was leaving the room. The only person with a credible reason to be in Alex's room at this point in the show was the wardrobe person.

Her skin tingled as she watched creepy Frank look both ways before he silently closed the door. Why was Frank in Alex's room?

As head of security, he was supposed to verify that the guards were in place to prevent anyone from sneaking backstage during the intermission.

Danni's pulse sped as Frank headed toward her hiding place. She held her breath and squeezed into the narrow space behind the speaker. The crowd's shouts for more when the set ended was background noise to her fast-beating heart reverberating in her eardrums. Instead of holding her breath while smashed against the wall, she could have pretended she was returning to Alex's room. Except this wasn't the way that she would have come.

She was glad that she didn't wear heavy perfume since Frank strolled right past her without noticing. She wiggled out of her hiding spot and headed to Alex's room. Could Frank be the stalker?

Her brain went into hyperdrive. Despite not liking the way Frank stared at her, she couldn't think of one reason for Frank to sabotage Alex. The man was supposedly his friend and provided Frank's income. How did Alex ending his tour early benefit Frank? She needed to find out. Lucky Reeves Hewitt, IT wizard for Jenkins Security, was her bestie.

All this skulking around gave her a little thrill, but nothing like those Jenkins boys and their friends. And even though her plans to sleep with Alex had gone by the wayside, she still wanted to prove her strength and smarts. People might focus on her looks, but she knew where her true power lay. And taking down this stalker would fulfill her real desire—to prove just how kick-ass and capable she was. Then maybe it would be time to join Jenkins Security. Or maybe the FBI…

Mission: Impossible to Protect is available in ebook and paperback from your favorite online retailer.

Enjoy an excerpt from

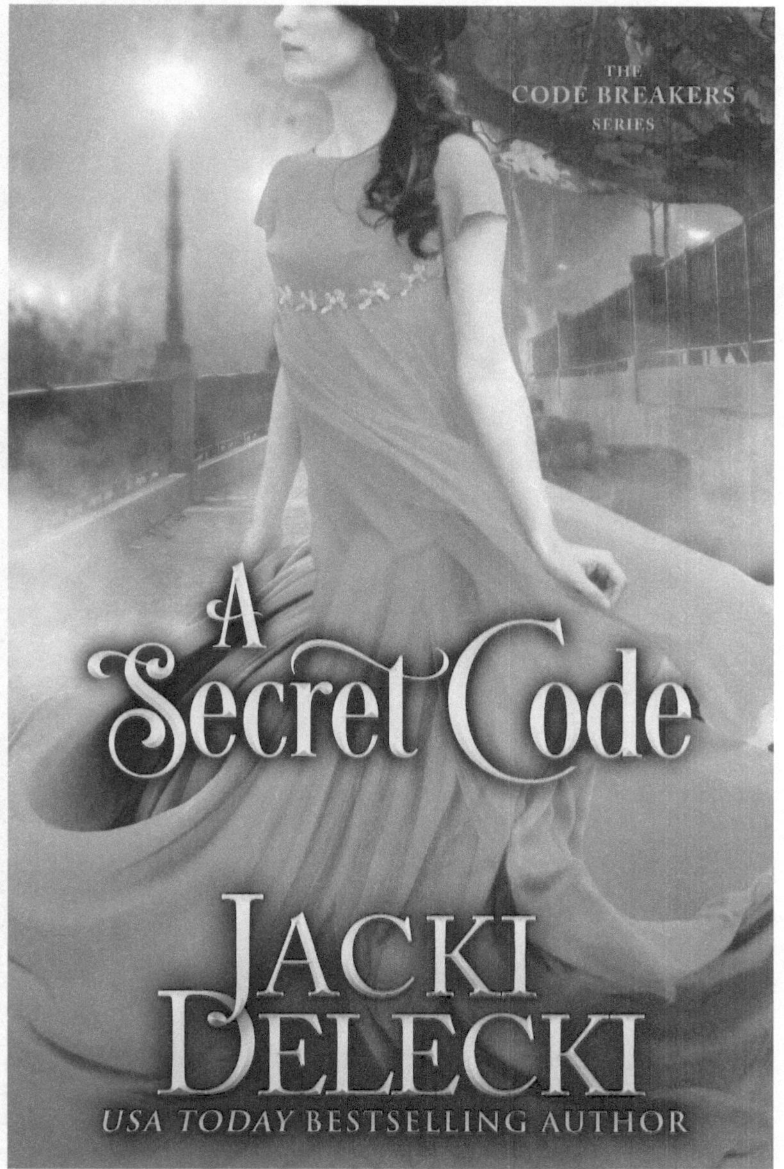

THE
CODE BREAKERS
SERIES
A
Secret Code
JACKI
DELECKI
USA TODAY BESTSELLING AUTHOR

Joie shifted her weight trying to remain still not to move her feet and raise suspicion as she stood behind the screen in the ladies' retiring room. It was time for everyone to make their way back to the ball. Didn't the two stragglers hear the orchestra warming up? It would be just her luck that the two chattering women had no partners for the next set. How much longer before the room was empty, and she could sneak down the hall?

Fortunately, there was more than one chamber pot for the use of all the ladies at the ball. Otherwise, her plan of making her way to the servants' quarters in Rathbourne house would never work. She counted to ten again and steeled herself for patience.

"She sailed into the ball as if everyone would have forgotten her scandalous behavior with Lord Ayer."

The top of Joie's ears burned at the mention of the despicable lord. Could there be more than one woman compromised by Lord Ayer? He was enough of a scoundrel to have lured another innocent woman to the conservatory. If there was another victim of Lord Ayer's malicious behavior Joie would wish to console the poor woman.

"She acts oblivious… As if everyone isn't talking about the daughter of an archbishop caught in a compromising situation."

Drat. They must be talking about her since there couldn't be another archbishop's daughter who Lord Ayer tried to kiss. None of the high ranking clergy had a daughter taking in the season.

There were all older like her father. She had been a surprise for her childless elder parents.

"Did you see the color of her dress? You would expect after her scandal that she would avoid drawing attention to herself."

The two tittered.

Joie tried to peak through the crack in the screen to see who the women were.

"Blue and orange. Who would ever wear those two colors?"

The blue silk was closer to a blue-gray; the orange was the color of a muted sunset in a winter sky. Had they not read La Belle Assemblée? The blue was called Turkish Blue and was the rage in Paris. She had always fantasized about living in Paris, feeling more of an affinity for French fashion and art like her mother than the staid sartorial tastes of the English. Not anymore. After tangling with French spies, she was ready to fight against her grandparent's homeland. Her mother would have supported Joie's decision.

"She's supposedly brought Lieutenant Talley up to snuff, but her father has rejected his offer. Everyone had already given up any hope of ever landing him and his large inheritance since he has never shown any interest in decent women—probably why his excellency rejected him."

"I'd love that man in my bed. He is such a large, delicious specimen."

One of the women snorted.

"It explains his attraction to her, doesn't it? She dresses like one of his paramours."

Joie smiled. She hoped that Reggie found her daring and as exciting as his opera dancers. Her recent dreams involved more than kisses with the enthralling and ardent man. She was limited in her imagination of exactly how the bedding occurred but she wanted more—more of his touches, more of everything.

"Like all of us, she will marry her father's choice."

Joie wanted to shout "never." She would elope before she would marry Albert.

"I can't blame her for dallying with Lieutenant Talley before her marriage. Who could resist that man in his dress regiments?"

She wasn't dallying with Reggie. All they had indulged so far was kisses—heated kisses burned into her skin and heart. She was more than ready to dally, but he continued to behave like a gentleman.

A Secret Code is available in ebook formats
from your favorite online retailer.

Jacki Delecki is a *USA Today* bestselling romantic suspense author whose stories are filled with heart-pounding adventure, danger, intrigue, and romance.

Her books have consistently received rave reviews for her three bestselling suspense series: Contemporary romantic suspense The Impossible Mission Series, featuring Special Force Operatives; The Grayce Walters Series, contemporary romantic suspense following a Seattle animal acupuncturist with a nose for crime; and The Code Breakers Series, Regency suspense set against the backdrop of the Napoleonic Wars.

Jacki's stories reflect her lifelong love affair with the arts and history. When not writing, she volunteers for Seattle's Ballet and Opera Companies, and leads children's tours of Pike Street Market.

To learn more about Jacki and her books and to be the first to hear about giveaways join her newsletter found on her website.

http://www.JackiDelecki.com

www.ingramcontent.com/pod-product-compliance
Lightning Source LLC
Chambersburg PA
CBHW050139110726
47898CB00008B/2597